A Captive

Heart

BASED ON
A TRUE STORY

Joyce Dent Morgan

ISBN 978-1-7376056-0-7 (paperback)
ISBN 978-1-7376056-1-4 (hardcover)
ISBN 978-1-7376056-2-1 (eBook)

All scripture is from the 1599 Geneva Bible

This is a work of fiction. All of the characters, names, incidents, organizations, and dialogue in this novel are either the products of the author's imagination or are used fictionally.

To my loving husband who has loved me for
more than half a century and will spend eternity
in Heaven with me where we will get to meet
the captives and hear the rest of the story.

"Keep thine heart with all diligence: for thereout cometh life."

Proverbs 4:23

List of Characters

Deerfield Residents

Hoyt Family

Sarah 17
Deacon and Lieutenant David Hoyt, Sarah's father
Abigail, Sarah's mother
Jonathan 15, Ebenezer 7, Benjamin 11, David early 20's,
Sarah's brothers
Mary and Abigail, Sarah's sisters

Nims Family

Ebenezer 17
Godfrey, Ebenezer's father
Mehitable, Ebenezer's stepmother
John, Ebenezer's older brother who was captured in earlier raid
Zebediah, Ebenezer's step-brother captured in earlier raid
Henry, Ebenezer's older brother

Abigail 4, Mary, and Mercy 5, Hittie 7, Ebenezer's sisters
Elizabeth Hull, Ebenezer's stepsister
Rebecca Mattoon and Thankful Munn, Ebenezer's married sisters
Phillip Mattoon and Benjamin Munn, Ebenezer's sisters' husbands

Williams family

Reverend John Williams, Deerfield's pastor
Eunice, wife of John Williams
Stephen, John, sons
Eunice, Esther, daughters
Stephen, John, sons
Eunice, Esther, daughters

Alexander Family

Captain Joseph Alexander, Sarah's betrothed
Lt. David Alexander, Joseph's father
Mary, Joseph's mother
Mary, Joseph's sister

Stebbins Family

Benoni, Godfrey Nims' youthful partner in crime
Abigail, Benoni's wife
Abigail, their daughter and friend of Sarah Hoyt

Jacques de Noyon, young Abigail's husband

Other Deerfield Residents

Elizabeth Price, Sarah's friend
The Indian Andre Stevens, Elizabeth Price's husband
Ebenezer Warner, wife Waitstill, and daughters Mary and Waitstill
Margaret Matoon, Ebenezer Nims' brother-in-law's sister
Judah Wright, Garrison soldier who later married Mary Hoyt
James Bennet, Godfrey Nims' youthful partner in crime
Jacob Hickson, Garrison soldier taken with Lt. Hoyt by Pennacocks
Mary Sheldon, daughter Remembrance, daughter-in-law Hannah
Joseph Petty, Martin Kellogg, Thomas Baker, escaped with John Nims

Men Active in Securing Release of Captives

Ensign John Sheldon, Captain Wells, Daniel Belden, Joseph Bradley
Reverend Stoddard, pastor of Northampton
Captains John Livingston and Samuel Vetch
Joseph Dudley, Governor of Massachusetts Bay Colony
William Dudley, son of Governor Dudley
Lieutenant Samuel Williams

Other Characters

Tsawenhohi, Great chief of the Hurons
Thaovenhosen, Huron captor
Jean-Baptiste Hertel de Rouville, Leader of army of French and Indians
Father Louis d'Avaugour, priest of Lorette
Captain Baptiste (aka Pierre Maisonnat), French privateer
Governor Vaudreuil, Governor of New France
Father Meriel, priest of Montreal

Fictional Characters

- **Sah-teenk-kah,** Thaovenhosen's wife
- **Gassisowangen,** Huron captor
- **Hatironta and Kondiaronk,** Gassisowangen's daughters
- **Madame Charon,** French woman who sheltered Sarah, Jonathan, and Ebenezer at Fort Chambley
- **Ashutua,** Thaovenhosen's grandmother and Sarah's mistress
- **Hum-ishi-ma,** adopted great granddaughter of Ashutua
- **Madame Marguerite de la Rochelle,** Sarah's mistress in Montreal
- **Lieutenant Charles de la Rochelle,** Marguerite's husband

- **Lieutenant St. Germain,** French soldier who wants to marry Sarah
- **Marie**, barmaid

Chapter One

⁓

"Hear me speedily, O Lord, for my spirit faileth: hide not thy face from me, else I shall be like unto them that go down into the pit."

Psalms 143:7

New England frontier, Deerfield, Massachusetts early fall 1703

Seventeen year old Ebenezer Nims picked up the sizing tool so he could measure his friend Sarah Hoyt's foot for new shoes. The two of them had been fast friends since they were children. As she animatedly chatted about how excited she was about her friend Abigail's recent engagement to the mysterious and romantic French fur trader Jacques de Noyon who had left New France and settled in Deerfield, Ebenezer felt his face grow hot. He wiped his sweaty hands on his shirt.

How he wished he had the courage to court Sarah, whom he'd dreamed of marrying since they were children. He knew that he was not the type of person she fancied. After all, she was the beautiful daughter of a military leader in their frontier outpost. She had always been attracted to the dashing hero type and Ebenezer was certainly far from that. His only skills lie in being a farmer and a shoemaker like his father, but even his father had fought in many battles over the course of his life and was a leader in their small frontier village of Deerfield.

With a sigh, Ebenezer's thoughts then wandered to the danger that all in the small village were fearing since receiving news warning of a possible attack on their town. Just this past August, Governor John Winthrop of Connecticut had received a letter from Colonel Samuel Partridge, the military commander of the frontier militia, seeking an additional fifty or sixty men to protect the Connecticut River Valley settlements. Governor Winthrop had forwarded the letter to Massachusetts Governor Dudley, who had shared the letter with Sarah's father, Lieutenant David Hoyt, and others of their town militia.

Lieutenant Hoyt had told Ebenezer's father Godfrey that Colonel Partridge had received reports from three friendly Mohawk Indians that a hostile body of French and Indians were advancing on the English colonies from Quebec in New France. The colonel feared that Deerfield might have been their main target because of its strategic location on the Connecticut River, which had been used by the Indians as a main thoroughfare for centuries.

All of these thoughts were whirling through Ebenezer's head as Sarah chattered on. He wondered if their demoralized town would be prepared for an attack and feared that if it did happen, he would not be able to contribute much help in the defenses of the town as he was not very skillful with firearms. He so wanted to be the brave person that Sarah deserved to protect her in these difficult times.

Though he had often practiced shooting, he usually missed the target, unlike his older brother John and stepbrother Zebediah. He decided that he would ask his brothers to help him become better at shooting since the threats against the town were increasing. It wasn't that he couldn't learn, he thought, but he just hadn't really had an opportunity to prove himself a man as the others had. He had spent most of his time with his father learning the cordwainer trade making shoes for the village inhabitants while his brothers had been the ones to do the hunting. Now that he was old enough to train with the other men in the village when they would conduct military exercises four times a year, Ebenezer thought that perhaps he could learn to shoot better and win Sarah's heart.

So, with these thoughts blotting out Sarah's gushing talk about how romantic her friend's intended husband was, and being too shy to do anything but listen to her, he bent down to finish his measuring.

"I can't wait for my shoes to be finished so I can wear them to Abigail's wedding! I also just heard that Elizabeth Price is marrying the Indian, Andre Stevens. Can you believe that? Isn't that just the most exciting news?" she exclaimed. "All of my friends are marrying and I can't wait for my own wedding someday," she went on, not realizing the effect it had upon Ebenezer.

"I'd love to marry you!" Ebenezer thought. "But w*hat am I thinking?"* he chastised himself. *"I will never be able to express my feelings for her and she'll never know how much I care for her and how I dream of sharing my life with her!"* He wished he had his father Godfrey's daring adventurous spirit, but he was plagued by shyness and other than being able to express his feelings to his little sisters and other members of his family, he just didn't talk much to others. When it came to Sarah Hoyt, he just couldn't get the words out.

"Your new shoes, um, they should be ready in two weeks," he stammered. "Shall I bring them to you when they are finished?" he asked as he picked up his sizing tool and put it on the bench next to his awl, stretching pliers, and other tools he used in his work as a shoemaker.

"That would be kind of you, Ebenezer," Sarah answered as she slipped out the door.

Ebenezer loved learning the cobbler trade from his father Godfrey who was presently at a meeting with other men from the village, leaving him to take care of business that day. It was the first time he had been alone in the shop and was proud that his father trusted him to do the work on his own.

He stood at the window and fondly watched Sarah as she walked down the street towards her home just outside the north gate of the village, happily greeting friends and neighbors. She stopped and chatted with his brother-in-law Philip's sister Margaret before greeting Reverend Williams' pregnant wife Eunice. Skipping along beside the good-wife was her eight year old daughter also named Eunice followed by twelve year old Esther, who was carrying her year old brother John. They were just leaving Goody Warner's house, who was also expecting a little one in the winter and had two daughters, Sarah aged five and Waitstill aged three. It seemed to Ebenezer that all the women in the village were either carrying new babes in their arms or would be soon. It made him long for a family of his own someday.

He loved the way everyone in the village loved Sarah and she loved them. As he continued gazing out the window of his shop, he marveled at how her golden red hair reflected the sunlight that streamed through the leaves that were just starting to turn color this early fall afternoon. He could have stood watching her all the way to her house, dreaming of the day when he and Sarah would have a little family of their own, but just then his sisters, five year old twins Mary and Mercy and seven year old sister Hittie, short for Mehitable, burst into the room. He took one last look at Sarah just in time to see her stop and talk quite animatedly to Joseph, one of the captains in the town militia.

"What is she doing talking to him?" he wondered as he turned to hug his little sisters.

"Ebenezer, listen to our new song we learned in school today!" his sisters exclaimed, interrupting his thoughts.

"It's Psalm 100," said Mary.

"Will you help us do it with your hammer?" Mercy asked.

"Of course," he smiled as he picked up his cobbler's tool. Recently he had entertained them by keeping time to their songs that they had learned in school. "Are you ready to sing? Let's go then," he invited.

In sweet little voices that warmed his heart, his three little sisters sang as he tapped out the rhythm with his hammer. The twins danced around the room as they sang, and Hittie clapped her hands to the rhythm.

> ***"In God the LORD be glad and light.***
> ***Praise Him throughout the earth.***
> ***Serve Him and come before his sight***
> ***With singing and with mirth.***

Know that the LORD our God He is.
He did us make and keep.
Not we ourselves for we are His
Own fold and pasture sheep.
O, go into His gates, always
Give thanks within the same.
Within His courts set forth His praise
And laud His holy name.
For why: the goodness of the LORD
Forevermore doth reign.
From age to age throughout the world
His truth doth still remain. "

When they finished singing, his sisters clapped their chubby little hands and looked to him for approval.

"Thank you for sharing your new song with me, my sisters," he said as he gave them each a warm hug. "It was very nice, and one of my favorite songs. I remember when I learned that one when I was in school. It was from the book "The Whole Book of Psalms." I remember our schoolmaster telling us that this version that we just sang was composed by a man named Simon Stubbs way back in 1621, even before our parents were born, and we still sing it today. He told us that they took the Psalms from the Bible and put them into meter form so that we could sing them in our meetings on the Sabbath. Perhaps we can sing it in our meeting one Sabbath day soon. I will speak to Reverend Williams when I next see him. Now, why don't you go share them with Mother and

7

little Abigail while I work on these new shoes for our friend Sarah Hoyt?" he said as he went to the shelf where the leather for shoes was stored.

"Will they have pretty buckles on them?" Hittie asked.

"Of course! What a great idea!" he answered as he gave her another hug.

Each of his little sisters smiled and skipped away to find their mother in the kitchen cutting up newly picked apples for a snack. With a full heart Ebenezer listened to them singing their new song as he began the task, nay the privilege, of making new shoes for his beloved Sarah.

"I'm going to do it," he sighed as his thoughts drifted back to her. "I'm going to ask her if I may court her. I've always wanted to marry Sarah and I'm just going to gather up my courage and ask her! We could be married after she turns eighteen on her birthday in May." He hummed the song that his sisters had shared with him and picked up his shoemaking tools and began to work.

He worked many days and many nights by firelight to make the most beautiful shoes he could using the best leather, adorning them with silver buckles for his Sarah. In just two weeks on October 8th, they were finished to perfection. His father Godfrey even told him they were the finest shoes he'd ever seen when Ebenezer proudly showed them to him. Wrapping them in a deerskin cloth, he headed out and walked towards the north gate to Sarah's house trying to work up the courage to ask her if she would let him court her.

"I can do this, Lord, if you will go before me," he prayed as he passed the Meeting House on his way there.

He tried to avoid the eyes of the town gossips as he travelled north through the town. He never knew what they were thinking and could only guess what they thought of him as he walked by carrying his bundle. When he reached his destination, Ebenezer paced back and forth in front of Sarah's house, which was just outside the village, rehearsing over and over the words he would say before finally summoning up enough courage to knock on her beautifully carved front door.

Saying another quick prayer, he hailed the house. He hoped desperately that Sarah would be the one to greet him there, but to his dismay, her father David Hoyt, not only one of the three Lieutenants in the town's militia but also one of the two deacons in their Puritan Church, opened the door and invited him inside.

"Come in, Ebenezer, Sarah is here with Captain Joseph Alexander," he said in greeting. "Sarah has just agreed to marry him when she turns eighteen next May. You know Joseph, don't you? He's the son of Lieutenant Alexander and a captain of our town militia. With all of the rumors of an impending attack by the Indians most of the young men are preparing to defend ourselves. I'm sure you are also training, are you not?"

"Did you say that Sarah is going to… *marry* him?" he stammered, ignoring Sarah's father's question about training to defend the town.

Ebenezer again felt ashamed that he didn't even know how to fire a weapon, never having accompanied his father and brothers on hunting expeditions. How he wished that he hadn't been content to stay back home and take care of his stepmother and younger siblings while the others travelled out in search of meat or looking for evidence of Indians who might be planning on attacking their village! How could he have been so stupid to think that he had any chance of marrying Sarah? Naturally she would be attracted to someone who could protect her from the many dangers of the frontier, just as he had feared.

Choking back tears he asked, "Could you just give these shoes to Sarah for me?" Ebenezer needed to avoid having to see Sarah with the dashing Captain Alexander. He knew that all the young unmarried girls in town were fawning over the captain. He just couldn't believe that Alexander would be asking Sarah to marry him, for hadn't he often been seen in the company of Margaret, his sister Rebecca's husband's sister? Everyone thought that they would marry and Ebenezer was stunned at this shocking announcement.

"Sarah must have already known that Joseph was going to ask for her hand in marriage that day that I saw her talking to him," he realized. *"How could I be so blind and naive,"* he lamented.

"Well, won't you at least come in and let me give you your pay for the shoes?" the deacon asked, interrupting his thoughts.

"Oh, no, Deacon Hoyt. You can pay my father later. I must… I must… um, I have to get back to work. Good day to you, Sir."

Ebenezer stumbled down the stairs, shaking and feeling his legs go numb. He couldn't catch his breath as struggled to hold back tears. He wiped them away with cold, sweaty hands.

"How could I have ever hoped that someone as exquisite as Sarah Nims, the deacon's beautiful daughter would be interested in someone like me?" he kept saying to himself as he wandered aimlessly through the town.

He couldn't go back to his house just yet; he was too embarrassed to face his father whom he told that morning about his intentions with Sarah. Godfrey and his step-mother Mehitable had joyously given their approval for Ebenezer to court Sarah. He just wasn't ready to face them with the disappointing news that his beloved Sarah had chosen another more handsome and dashing man to marry.

Not caring where he was going, he continued walking through the town kicking up the fallen leaves. He passed the Meeting House and then made his way to the Old Burying ground where his mother, baby sister Rebecca, brother Thomas, and step-brother Jeremiah who had died when he was trapped inside their burning house were buried. He ended up back outside the stockade trying to catch his breath and stop his shaking. Coming to the hill above the meadow where his family and other villagers pastured their cows, he sat down and tried to calm his fast beating heart.

Thinking he would find solace in this place where he often would go to think and pray, he was shocked to see his older brother John and step-brother Zebediah Williams being bound and taken away on horseback by a group of Indians. Was the dreaded Indian attack suddenly upon them? He wished that he could have done something to rescue them, but he knew it was useless for him to carry a firearm when he knew that he would probably miss his target even if he did try to fire a weapon.

Feeling defenseless, he realized that he would be captured as well if they saw him there, so he crept away from their sight and then quickly ran back to the town and burst into his house yelling for his father, Godfrey, to help. He knew that after all the grief his father had experienced in his life including many skirmishes with the Indians that he would be terribly distressed at the news of his sons' capture.

He had no horse to pursue the Indians, and feared that they would slay his sons if anyone chased them down, so Godfrey went to the townspeople and pleaded for help, but no one was willing to take the risk in fear of themselves being killed or captured. They all ran back to their own homes to prepare for any oncoming attack.

"I am being punished for my youthful sins!" Godfrey lamented. "Will my grief never end?"

"*His youthful sins*," Ebenezer mused. He recalled the story his father had shared with him just yesterday as he worked on finishing Sarah's shoes while his father repaired some shoes for his long-time friend and neighbor Benoni Stebbins.

"When Benoni, James Bennet and I were young lads just a few years younger than you are, Ebenezer," his father recalled, "an Indian from New France came to our town and we, being impressionable lads, were intrigued by the stories he told of his life there. I was an orphan in Northampton at the time and believed that my father, a French Huguenot, might be living there. You see, when I was just a young boy, about your sister Hittie's age, I remember that he and my mother often discussed going to New France to escape persecution by the Catholics in control of our country. A number of families from our area had done so."

"King Louis XIV had revoked the Edict of Nantes that had been issued in 1598 by King Henry IV. This law had given us Huguenots freedoms to worship as Protestants in the Catholic nation and was written in order to avoid religious wars."

"The Edict had given us civil rights which were also revoked by King Louis XIV. When the Edict was revoked many French Protestants left France for neighboring countries and my parents, your grandparents, fled to England. They had planned on sailing from there to the English colonies or to New France. Since my mother was expecting a child, my parents decided that my father would go ahead with the first group of people going to the new world and find a suitable place for us to live. My mother would follow in another voyage with me and the new baby once she was able to travel," Godfrey's father had explained.

"But, what happened? Didn't your plans work out?" Ebenezer had asked.

"No, much to my dismay and grief after looking forward to the adventure of making a new home in a place that would be accepting to us, my mother died in childbirth. I was left alone and decided to sell all of our household goods and also worked on the ship to have enough money for passage on a ship bound for Boston. I thought I could find my way to my father from there, but I didn't even know where to find him. After many years of searching in the Boston area, I went with a group of settlers to Northampton who said that perhaps we would find him there as many of them had heard that there were some French Huguenots living in the area."

"After arriving in Northampton," his father continued, "I discovered that my father wasn't there and that he may have travelled to New France with a group of French speaking emigrants from our home town of Nimes, France."

"Is that why our name is 'Nims'?" Ebenezer interrupted.

"Yes, my real name is Godefroi de Nimes, but I changed the spelling before I came to the Massachusetts Bay colony because I wanted to have a more English sounding name in order to gain passage on an English ship, even though I spoke only a little English that I had learned when we moved to England. On board the ship I learned more of the language to get by in the English colony."

"Tell me about the Indian and what happened to you and the other boys," Ebenezer prodded.

"He was a vagrant Indian called Queciuelett from New France who spoke French. Because I was able to understand him, I asked him if he would guide me to New France where I could look for my father. He readily agreed if I would pay him a large sum of wampum. I talked my friends James Bennet and Benoni Stebbins into joining me in my quest and persuaded them to help me rob some of the villagers while they were at the Public Meeting House on the Sabbath. I don't know why I made them take part in my plan. Since I was not a Puritan at that time, I didn't attend Sabbath meetings with the rest of the villagers. Benoni and James faked illnesses in order to be excused from attendance at the meeting. I am ashamed of what I did now, but at the time it seemed the only choice I had. They thought that it would be a great adventure."

"But were you successful?" Ebenezer asked. "Did you ever find your father?"

"No, unfortunately, or I should say, 'fortunately' as it turned out, we were caught by the town constable and sent to court in Springfield where we confessed our crimes and were sentenced to pay a fine and also were whipped. Because I was the oldest and the ringleader, I was given a more severe punishment, but the experience made me realize the folly of my actions. I had great respect for the constable and wanted to change my ways. I repented of my sins and left Northampton a few years later and was one of the first settlers here in Deerfield.

"Since there was no housing available and as winter was coming on, I made a crude shelter that first year by digging a kind of cellar home in the hill just across the way from where our house is now. You may remember that I once showed it to you. I was proud to serve in my new community and took the Oath of Fidelity to the colony, giving up my allegiance to the Huguenot faith of my parents and joining the Puritan Society. I soon became the town constable in order to honor the constable from Northampton who helped me change my ways. Later I was elected as selectman of the village. I then realized that I would probably never find my father, but I was content to make a new life in Deerfield and serve my new community. I met and married your mother Mary who was a widow with two children at the time. Then we had John, Henry, Thankful and you. As you know, your mother died when you were just a baby and a few years later I married your step-mother who raised you like her own and loves you all dearly."

"I do think of her as my mother as I don't even remember my other mother," Ebenezer shared. "I've always felt that she's loved all of us as if we were her own children."

"Yes, she does. She is a good woman and we are all blessed to have her," his father agreed.

As Ebenezer pondered these words of the day before, he realized that his father might end up going to New France all these years later not to look for his father, but perhaps now to search for his two sons if he could only have some help from the colonial government. Ebenezer dreamed of being able to help in the search for his brothers.

Little did Ebenezer know what other events would forever change the course of his and his family's life.

Chapter Two

—— ❧ ——

"I have called upon thee: surely thou wilt hear me, O God: incline thine ear to me, and hearken unto my words.

Show thy marvelous mercies: thou that art the Savior of them that trust in thee, from such as resist thy right hand.

Keep me as the apple of the eye: hide me under the shadow of thy wings, From the wicked that oppress me, from mine enemies, which compass me round about for my soul."

Psalms 17:6-9

A few weeks later on his way to a meeting at the Meeting House with the men of the village where they were discussing what to do about rescuing his brothers and preparing for an attack on their village, Ebenezer overheard Sarah telling her friends that she and Joseph Alexander would be married after her birthday in May. Ebenezer hung back and said nothing, briefly smiling weakly at Sarah as she looked over to where he was standing in the shadows of a huge oak tree across from the Meeting House.

"That could have been me she was talking about marrying," he lamented. *"I should have asked for her hand sooner and not been such a coward!"*

"Ebenezer, hurry up! The meeting is about to get started," his older brother Henry called, interrupting his musings. "We need to be there to support Father in his request for help to get Zebediah and John back. You know that we will be fined a shilling if we do not attend the meeting."

He nodded and joined the rest of the men entering the Meeting House. Reverend Williams opened in prayer and then listened as Ebenezer's father begged the others for help.

"As you know, we have all suffered losses the past several years, some of us barely missing being slain or captured ourselves," Godfrey began. "I have lost a wife and children and now two of my sons are captured and must be suffering unspeakable sufferings. My wife is inconsolable and we must do something to bring them back," he cried.

"We must petition Governor Dudley to try and negotiate a ransom for them," Ensign John Sheldon suggested.

"I would if I had the money," Godfrey lamented.

"You could apply for a relief from your taxes this year in order to save the money for their ransom," suggested his childhood friend Benoni Stebbins. "I have heard from others who were successful in being granted such relief."

Godfrey thanked them and said he would consider doing what they suggested and the men continued with their discussion.

"We must also ask for help from the governor to have money to enlarge our stockade so that those who live outside the palisades will be protected from any attacks," Sarah's father Lieutenant Hoyt suggested. "My home is outside the walls, but if we could enlarge the fort and place it inside the walls, it would be a good, secure place for all the other people who live further out to find refuge should an attack happen. We may need to have spaces to house any soldiers that might be sent to help in our defense."

"That's a great idea," David Alexander, Sarah's Joseph's father, agreed.

The men came to the consensus that they would begin by moving those outside the fort into homes within the existing walls and build temporary shelters for those who had no place to go inside the palisade.

Benjamin Munn, Ebenezer's sister Thankful's husband, spoke up, "My wife and I can move into the temporary shelter her father lived in when he first came to Deerfield some thirty years ago. We can fix it up and make it livable until we can move back to our home or build something more permanent. That will leave room for any militia that come to help us to live in others' homes."

Reverend Williams then assigned Captain Wells, Lieutenant Hoyt, Ensign John Sheldon and Daniel Belden to be in charge of the endeavor until they could hear back from the governor.

Then he led them in prayer before they broke into smaller groups and made plans for enlarging the stockade.

The pastor left the meeting and wrote a letter to Governor Dudley, asking him for funds to expand their fort, explaining that the settlers were having to leave their homes and move into the ten homes within the existing fort for protection from an imminent attack. He told how the farmers were fearful of leaving the fort to tend their fields for fear of attack or capture. He explained that the people would have been willing to pay their taxes, but were living in extreme poverty because they couldn't harvest their crops. He ended with a plea for the governor and Assembly to take pity and compassion on the distressed parents of the two captives and make an effort to negotiate a prisoner exchange for their release.

All of those who had been gathered at the meeting went back to their homes to gather axes and tools to cut down trees on the hillside just outside the village and across the meadows where they pastured their livestock. They crossed the cow pasture where Ebenezer's brothers had been before being taken just a few months before. After cutting the trees and stripping off bark, they hauled them back to the village where they enlarged and reinforced the palisade. Then Sarah's family and several others moved into crude temporary shelters inside the village or stayed with friends or family members there. Once all the residents had moved inside the palisades, they waited anxiously for the dreaded attack.

As the fall turned to winter the townspeople grew even more nervous as they feared further attacks by Indians. Most of them were farmers and only a few of them were skilled hunters. Ebenezer struggled to master the use of his father's flintlock, but was still not very successful in hitting a target. He continued to worry that he would not be able to be of much help should he be required to shoot an enemy attacker to help protect his family and neighbors, but he was determined to do all he could to help those who lived in his village.

He temporarily forgot his grief over Sarah in this fear of further Indian attacks when he was summoned with the rest of the men in town to another town meeting in February. All of the men gathered in the Meeting House and sat dreading the announcement that they all knew was coming. Ebenezer looked to his father, who was pale and stricken with grief over his unsuccessful attempts to rescue John and Zebediah, who had now been missing for more than four months. He listened to murmurs by the men and could hear the fear in their voices. Sarah's father Lieutenant Hoyt lifted his hand for silence and the room grew quiet. The men took their seats on the hard benches and waited for him to speak.

Clearing his throat, Hoyt began to speak to his fellow citizens. "Men of Deerfield, we must prepare for an imminent attack. We've received reports of more possible French and Indian raids coming to the Connecticut Valley. We don't know when the attack will come, but Governor Dudley says that news has arrived from New York's Indian agent Pieter Schuyler that the French and Indians have already attacked villages in southern Maine and are headed our way. Governor Dudley has heeded our pleas and promised to send men from the militia to help defend us."

The town's residents had been fearing further attacks since receiving the news from Colonel Partridge in August and then the capture of John Nims and Zebediah Williams earlier that fall, but now it seemed that the dreaded attack was finally coming. Then, on February 24th, 1704 in an answer to Reverend Williams letter that preceding fall, twenty militia arrived in Deerfield and were garrisoned inside the newly fortified town.

Later that week heavy snows covered the town, burying clearings, meadows, and the frozen river. Ebenezer and his father trudged through the woods, gathering firewood and loading it into their ox-driven cart. When they came back into the village, they smiled at some of the young boys throwing snowballs at each other. They brought the firewood to the barn and unloaded it before feeding the cattle, pigs, and horses sheltered there. His sisters were there milking the cow for the night's meal of mush and milk. Outside the house, Ebenezer's mother was just drawing a pail of water with the help of a long well sweep.

"Tomorrow we must bring some corn, wheat, and meat to Reverend Williams for our tithe," Godfrey reminded his son before the family went inside to prepare for the night.

On that same night of February 28th, Deacon Hoyt and his family gathered around the fire in their crude temporary shelter made of rough hewn logs with dried leaves stuffed between the cracks and then plastered over with mud hauled from the nearby river. The windows were not of glass as they had in their former house outside the stockade, but rather of oiled paper.

As he picked up the treasured family Bible that had been passed down from his grandfather Simon who had brought it from England in 1628, Deacon Hoyt looked fondly at his beautiful, blue-eyed, 44 year old wife Abigail, sons Ebenezer age nine, Benjamin age eleven, and Jonathan age fifteen, and daughters Abigail age two and Sarah age seventeen. His oldest daughter Mary was visiting a friend in the nearby village of Hatfield.

All of his other children had their mother's sky blue eyes and straight flaxen colored hair, but Sarah took after her father with her wavy hair the color of a fox and eyes sometimes the color of summer leaves and other times the color of an azure sky. Although her brothers and sisters all had their mother's fair skin, Sarah's was the color of fresh cream. Her nose was dotted with freckles like her beloved father's.

Although he loved all of his children, Deacon Hoyt favored Sarah, and called her his "Little Fox." Perhaps because she shared his features, or more likely, because of her deep, unshakable faith in God and spirited nature, she had a special place in his heart. Recently he had been spending much time with her because of her pending marriage to the twenty-two year old Joseph Alexander.

He was somewhat surprised that she had agreed to marry the man. He had always thought that Sarah would marry his friend Godfrey Nims' son Ebenezer as the two had spent so much time together as children. He had always enjoyed watching them as they would sing together under the maple trees in the summer, joyfully sharing Psalms they had learned in school. He thought that shy Ebenezer would be a good balance for his spirited daughter who was sometimes inclined to make rash decisions.

But now Sarah was planning on being married when she turned eighteen on her birthday in May, just three months away. Deacon Hoyt knew that she was anxious to be married and have children. He was just surprised that she had chosen the impulsive Joseph as her intended husband. Because Joseph was a soldier and captain in the town's militia, Deacon Hoyt feared that Sarah was enamored with his status and caught up in the romance of being married to a dashing young soldier. He hoped they would be happy and knew that he would have to trust God for not only their happiness, but their survival if the feared attack took place.

Pondering all of these things, Deacon Hoyt opened the treasured family Bible and began reading from the book of Psalms.

> *"When I cry unto thee, then shall*
> *mine enemies turn back: this I know;*
> *for God is for me. In God will I praise*
> *his word: in the Lord will I praise his*
> *word. In God have I put my trust: I will*
> *not be afraid of what man can do unto*
> *me. "*

Closing the sacred book he led his family in prayer. As they prepared to retire for the night, Sarah asked her father, "Do you think we will be safe at least until spring, until my wedding to Captain Alexander? I am afraid, father, that we will not be able to survive an attack should it really happen."

Moving closer to her and taking her hand in his, he tried to assure her. "We should be alright for now," he sighed. "The French and Indians don't usually attack in the dead of winter, but we still must be on our guard. The logistics of such an attack this time of year would be formidable. The men in the town have been training with their muskets to fight off any attackers should they come."

Turning to the rest of his family he tried to assure them. "As you all know, each night one of the garrison soldiers stands guard and watches for anything that might indicate an attack is forthcoming. The guard will sound the alarm so that we will be ready to defend ourselves. Let us retire now, knowing that God will protect us. Don't be afraid."

Sarah kissed her mother and father goodnight and made her way to the far corner of the room where she had been sleeping behind a muslin curtain strung on a cord tied between the rafters since they abandoned their beautiful home outside the palisade. Because of the unusually bitter cold that night, she dressed warmly in woolen socks and slipped into her warmest chemise that had long, detachable sleeves, and after brushing her hair, she braided it into one long braid and tied her woolen nightcap under her chin. Reaching into the lovely, ornately carved chest at the foot of her bed which she had brought from their home, she took out the new quilt that she and her mother and sister Mary had recently finished in preparation for her coming wedding. She caressed it lovingly, dreaming of the day it would be used to cover her and her handsome husband after they were married. Before snuffing out her candle, she picked up her Psalter and read the following verses from Psalm 17:

"I have called upon thee: surely thou wilt hear me, O God: incline thine ear to me, and hearken unto my words. Show thy marvelous mercies: thou that art the Savior of them that trust in thee, from such as resist thy right hand. Keep me as the apple of the eye: hide me under the shadow of thy wings,

> **From the wicked that oppress me, from
> mine enemies, which compass me round
> about for my soul.***"*

Then extinguishing the candle that she and her mother had just finished dipping that day, she snuggled under her quilts and felt comforted as she settled in for the night on her bed made of logs with ropes tied across the beams and covered with bags of straw and covered with sheets of homespun muslin. She wondered if she would ever again sleep in a four-poster bed with a feather mattress like she had in her former home. She listened to the quiet breathing of her mother and siblings and the soft snoring of her father on the other side of the muslin curtain. She soon drifted off to sleep, dreaming of her beloved Joseph and her wedding just three months away.

But, little did she know the terrors that would awaken her in the early dawn the next morning.

Chapter Three

"He lieth in wait in the villages;
in the secret places doth he
murder the innocent; his eyes
are bent against the poor.

He lieth in wait secretly, even as a
lion in his den; he lieth in wait to
spoil the poor; he doth spoil the poor,
when he draweth him into his net.

He croucheth and boweth; therefore
heaps of the poor do fall by his might."

Psalms 10:8-10

Jean-Baptiste Hertel de Rouville and his army of about fifty Frenchmen and two hundred Indians from five tribes united at Fort Chambly near Montreal more than two hundred fifty miles north of Deerfield to begin their raid. It had been months in the planning and was now coming to fruition. He thought about the various reasons why the attack would happen.

The French wanted to destroy property of the English and kill as many as they could before returning to New France as quickly as possible. England and France were fighting The War of Spanish Succession, known as Queen Anne's War in the colonies, in Europe. An even more compelling reason for the French government to attack the remote outpost of Deerfield was because they desired to have a prominent captive that they could exchange for the famous French pirate Pierre Maisonnat dit Baptiste who had been captured by the English at the start of Queen Anne's War and was being held captive in a Boston prison. Governor de Vaudreuil of New France knew that the town's Puritan pastor, Reverend Williams, was a perfect choice as a captive as he was related to the famous Reverends Cotton and Increase Mather of Boston.

He knew that in the past whenever England and France were at war, Governor Dudley of the Massachusetts Bay Colony would gather the Abenaki chiefs together to assure that they would have peace during the European wars. The governor had met with these chiefs in June of 1703 and they had promised that they would not attack the English settlements. Despite their promises to the Massachusetts Bay governor, de Rouville was delighted that Canada's Governor de Vaudreuil had secretly gathered more than 500 Abenakis to strike several settlements in Maine and elsewhere in the colonies.

He knew that the Indians—Abenakis, Hurons, Kahnawake Mohawks, Pennacooks, and Iroquois of the Mountain, had different motives for their involvement in the raid. They accompanied the French as allies, not subjects, because of their common faith as Catholics, and because the French offered to pay them as compensation for time lost for hunting and gathering furs. De Vaudreuil felt confident that they would have a successful raid with the help of these Indians.

But the five tribes involved in this raid had an even more compelling and ominous reason to join in the fight, and that was their desire to take captives in what was known as Mourning Wars. Some, especially women and children, the Indians wanted to adopt into their families to replace dead relatives, and others, especially men, for torture to avenge members of their tribe who had been killed in various battles with other tribes or with Englishmen. Even though the Indians were "praying Indians", as the English called them, they still held fast to their traditions of Mourning Wars.

Though the French and Indians didn't usually begin their attacks in the middle of winter, de Rouville wanted to have the element of surprise. He chose Deerfield because it was the westernmost outpost in the New England frontier and was populated mostly by farmers who were unaccustomed to battle. Also, it was strategically located along the Connecticut River, a main north-south thoroughfare used by Indians for centuries. There had been a few skirmishes between the various Indians and the Deerfield residents over the years, but none at the magnitude of this planned attack. The French governor anticipated a swift victory.

After travelling for many weeks through the frozen wilderness, the exhausted attackers cached most of their supplies in a camp about thirty miles north of the village and then made their way to a camp closer to the place of attack known as Petty's Plain about two miles from Deerfield. As the Deerfield inhabitants prepared for the night, Lieutenant Hertel de Rouville's men scouted the defenses of the town and noticed that because of a strong wind the previous day, the snow had accumulated in drifts against the walls of the palisade. Hurrying back to Lieutenant de Rouville, the scouts reported that the walls could easily be scaled by simply walking up the drifts and over the top.

"We attack before dawn!" the leader exclaimed. Pointing to several of the men, he commanded, "Scale the palisade and open the north gate. The rest of us will storm in and catch them unaware as they sleep. Kill as many men as you can and destroy the homes and buildings. Kill the livestock and take as much plunder as you can carry for our journey northward."

Tsawenhohi, the "Great Chief" of the Hurons of Lorette, a village near the town of Quebec, spoke up and commanded his warriors to take as many captives as they could, and the other chiefs agreed. The Hurons, as they were called by the French because of the French word for *"bristly haired knave,"* or the Wendat meaning *"villagers",* as they called themselves, were especially desirous of captives as they had suffered terrible losses in number in the preceding decades. They had been dispersed from their homeland by the Iroquois in 1650 and relocated to a new village, Lorette, near Quebec. Where they had formerly numbered between 35,000 and 40,000 members, after the devastating losses from their enemy and then even more deaths from epidemics of measles, smallpox, and influenza brought on by the French, this small band of the Hurons who were able to relocate to Lorette now numbered only about three hundred people. Most of them had been converted to Christianity by the Jesuits priests at the mission there in exchange for firearms to fight their Iroquois enemies.

As the Deerfield residents slept unawares, trusting in their *"faithful guard"* to warn them of any impending raiders, for whatever reason, the man who was on duty that night fell asleep at his post and was completely unaware of the impending horrors that were to overtake his town. Perhaps he had grown complacent believing that the enemy wouldn't travel the three hundred miles from Canada during this, the coldest time of year. How he would later regret this breach of the villagers' trust in him to keep them safe!

Two hours before dawn February 29, 1704 Lieutenant de Rouville and his men, cold and famished from their journey south, left their packs and snowshoes behind and crept cautiously over the crusted snow. De Rouville periodically ordered the men to stop so that the guards would mistake their sounds for simply the rising and falling of the wind. Hearing no alarm being sounded, de Rouville and his men mounted the palisade and crept silently over the wall.

The sleeping guard was not awakened until the French and Indians stormed into Deerfield and began attacking houses and buildings. He tried to fire two warning shots, but it was too late. With a sinking heart he could only watch as the Indians broke through doors with hatchets and ransacked the houses, taking items and food that they would need on their march northward as de Rouville commanded. They killed the livestock that they couldn't take with them and slew the townspeople that were of no value to them as captives, mostly men of fighting age, older women and young children too weak to make the treacherous march northward.

"God forgive me!" the distraught guard wept as he watched the town being laid waste. I have failed You and I have failed my duty to these precious people." He rushed blindly into the fray, trying to shoot the raiders, but missing them because his eyes were filled with tears and his arms were trembling uncontrollably.

Reverend Williams was startled awake by a crowd of Indians breaking down his door. He shouted to the two garrison soldiers who were in his house and then grabbed a pistol from the head of his bed and fired at the nearest Indian, a Kahnawake chief, but the weapon misfired. He was seized and bound and watched in horror as two of his children were murdered along with their Negro nurse named Parthena.

Meanwhile upstairs one of the lodgers named Stoddard grabbed a cloak, threw himself out the window and climbed the palisade, escaping half-naked into the snow. He stopped outside the palisade and tore strips of material from his cloak to bind his feet. Then he ran through the snow to the nearby village of Hatfield and summoned help from the sleeping villagers.

Chapter Four

"Hear my voice, O God, in my prayer: preserve my life from fear of the enemy."

Psalm 64:1

Screams, horrendous screams, shattered Sarah's dreams, turning them into nightmares that fateful early morning. Bolting upright in bed, she shivered as the shrieks grew louder and closer, piercing the predawn darkness. Gunshots rang through the village. Flames from burning houses lit up her window, choking her as she struggled to breathe. She realized now that some of the screams were coming from just behind the quilt which hung from the rafters of their house. She was too frightened to look to see what might be happening to her family.

Suddenly a bloodied face pulled back her curtain and hovered over her, causing her heart to start beating so loudly it almost drowned out the screams and gunshots. The frightful man was covered in black and red paint on his bare chest and face. His hair stood in stiff ridges that extended from his forehead to his neck. He jerked her from her warm bed and motioned for her to get dressed and follow him.

She trembled as she pulled some undergarments underneath her chemise and rummaged through the carved chest at the end of her bed for an extra pair of warm stockings. She hastily pulled them on and tied them as best as she could with her shaking hands. Next she found her petticoat hanging on a peg on the wall. She put that on and then came her homespun woolen bodice followed by her indigo colored waistcoat and matching skirt. She started to reach for her apron, but the attacker held his hatchet over her head and told her no. Then she reached for her lovely leather shoes with shiny buckles that Ebenezer had made for her in the fall and struggled to put them on with trembling hands, never letting her eyes waiver from watching the frightening figure who hovered over her and motioned for her to hurry.

Hardly being able to breathe, she grabbed her woolen cloak and hastily threw it over her shoulders. She had no time to fix her hair, but pushed some of the loose strands under her cap.

The hideous stranger dragged her through the curtain where she was confronted with the terrifying sight of her father David struggling against several Indian attackers while her mother, white-faced and dressed in only her muslin nightdress, nursed Sarah's wailing two-year-old baby sister Abigail to try and comfort and quiet her. Her brothers, Jonathan and Ebenezer, were futilely trying to ward off the attackers before being told to get dressed quickly.

The Indian attackers were pillaging the kitchen area, shoving food into their mouths and throwing items into one of the quilts they had ripped from her parents' bed. Sarah watched as they grabbed hams, dried fruit, loaves of bread, cooking utensils and her father's musket, powder and shot. They smashed her mother's beautiful china that had come from England and been handed down to her from her mother and her grandmother, and destroyed whatever they couldn't use. While the Indians were busy in the kitchen pillaging and filling their bellies, her wounded father grabbed the family Bible that had been such a comfort to them all just hours earlier and stuffed it in a purse which was attached to his belted leather breeches. He helped his wife dress while Sarah dressed her little sister Abigail.

"Has anyone seen Benjamin?" Sarah whispered to her father as she looked around the room.

He shook his head and said, "We must pray that he was not slain in his bed."

Then they were all seized, bound with leather cords and carried away up the hill to the Meeting House where they were met with other captives also bound and wounded. Sarah looked around to see if her brother Benjamin was there, but he was still missing. She wondered if he was already dead in his bed as her father had feared.

"Where is Joseph?" she wondered, scanning all the faces of all those being held in the Meeting House and not seeing her betrothed. As they waited in the red glare brought about by the burning of the homes in the village, Sarah leaned against her mother and wept silently, afraid that if she cried out, she would be brutally and unmercifully killed as she'd seen happen to many of her friends and neighbors on the way to the Meeting House.

Surrounded by men crying out in loud prayers to God to save them and women weeping for murdered children and spouses, Sarah remembered the verses from Psalm 56, the one her father had read before bed the night before, whispering them to her younger brothers Ebenezer and Jonathan.

Benjamin was still nowhere to be seen. She didn't know that on hearing the commotion going on all around him, he had jumped through a window in the back of the house and hidden in a corn crib until after the attackers left the village. Her older brother David, Jr. was not among the captives being held in the Meeting House. She hoped that he was one of the ones in Benoni Stebbins' house which was one of the houses that, because of its three foot thick fortified walls, was dedicated as a garrison house built to withstand attacks. She prayed that both brothers and Joseph were safe inside and fending off the attackers.

Glancing around the room, she was stunned to see her beloved pastor Reverend John Williams bloodied and wounded, comforting his distraught wife Eunice who was bent over in grief and calling the names of her babies, one month old Jerusa and one year old John, the ones who were brutally killed in the attack on their home which now was a pile of ashes. Around her was the moaning of the attackers who had been wounded in the skirmishes around the village. Babies were crying with hunger and cold, and children were shrieking in terror after seeing their beloved family members brutally murdered or wounded.

Reverend Williams rose with difficulty and spoke out above the fray and, choking back tears, he offered encouragement to his bereaved flock. "Beloved friends and neighbors, we must pray to our Lord that we would have grace to glorify His name, whether in life or death."

Sarah was relieved to finally meet the eyes of her betrothed, who was in a dark corner mourning the death of his two year old baby sister Mary, one of the first slain by the attackers. His mother sat next to him, but his father was not with them. Joseph was whispering to his mother Mary that he would escape and try to find out what had happened to his father who was probably still trying to fight off the attackers. He wanted to go to Sarah and offer her encouragement, but was not able to as one of the Indians grabbed him and forced him to gather with the rest of the men who were being separated from their wives and children.

Ebenezer Nims, also bound and wounded, was choking back tears as he mourned the violent death of his brother Henry who had been shot in the head by one of the French soldiers as he had struggled to escape. He was temporarily relieved to remember how he had quickly hidden his five year old twin sisters Mary and Mercy and seven year old Hittie in their cellar before the attackers broke into their home. Ebenezer had hastily covered the trap door with a hooked rug just before he was seized by a huge, terrifying Indian with evil looking paint covering his half-naked body and bound and led away to the Meeting House.

He hoped that if he was carried away as a captive, any surviving townspeople would rescue his sisters after the fighting was over. He tried to comfort his grieving step-mother and four-year-old sister Abigail who was screeching in fear. Their father Godfrey was nowhere to be seen. Had he been killed or had he miraculously escaped or been spared? Was he one of the ones who were outside fighting off the enemy? Had he made it safely to his friend Benoni Stebbins' house? It was one which was made bulletproof by a layer of bricks between the inner and outer walls with small windows and projecting upper story to make it more defensible. He hoped and prayed that it was so, but Ebenezer didn't know that it would be many years before he would learn the fate of his beloved father.

Surrounded by the moans and weeping of the survivors, Ebenezer thought of all that his father had gone through in his life. Not only had he lost the family members who lay in the Old Burying Ground and his son John and step-son Zebediah who may or may not still be alive in captivity, but over the years he had fought off many Indian attacks, barely escaping with his life.

Once when Ebenezer was just three years old, three Indians arrived in their town, saying that they wanted to trade. One of them named Chepasson when compelled to pay a debt that he owed to one of the townspeople berated the townspeople and called them all boys who were afraid to fight and would cry just like the Dutch did when the Frenchmen came and attacked New York. Then Chepasson threatened to cut off their neighbor Benjamin Brooks' head. He then said he wanted to obtain a gun and knife so he could kill Ebenezer's father Godfrey. After that the Indian was confined and placed under guard. One of the Negroes who worked for Reverend Williams, known by the name of Tigo, short for Santiago, refused to give him a knife or gun so he could kill Godfrey. The Indian attempted to pull a knife and gun from his guard, telling him that he would not harm him, but would only hurt the Englishman, Ebenezer's father. Tigo still refused. The next day Chepasson tried to bribe another one of the young men who was guarding him and when the boy refused, he overpowered him and stole the weapons. As he was running for the gate, he was shot dead, but Ebenezer's father was shaken with the whole episode.

Now Ebenezer faced this tragedy which would be almost impossible for him to bear. How he wished his father were here with him to lend what strength he could to those of his family who remained. Ebenezer realized that he would now be responsible for caring for the members of his family who now huddled together in the Meeting House awaiting their fate.

These thoughts consumed Ebenezer as he watched his stepmother and stepsister Elizabeth and other captives in the Meeting House wondering if they would be killed or taken captive. He saw the flames raging outside the window and prayed that his three young step sisters were not now lying in the ashes. He didn't know if his sister Thankful and her family who were in their crude home which was built so many years before by his father, dug out of the hillside and boarded over as a shelter when they moved inside the stockade, would be hidden enough by the deep snow surrounding it to keep them safe.

The enemy's casualties were stretched out on the hard benches near Ebenezer. The wounded leader of the massacre, Lieutenant Hertel de Rouville, rushed into the room to comfort one of his three wounded brothers who had accompanied him on the raid. Ebenezer heard him whisper curses against the Indians who had promised to fight like civilized

Frenchmen. "They weren't supposed to massacre the women and children," he groaned. "They were supposed to kill the men and capture the women and children!"

Hearing commotion and shots outside, Ebenezer realized that some of the villagers, perhaps his father, and garrisoned soldiers from neighboring towns were fighting back against the attack. He prayed that they would be victorious in fighting off the attackers and would be able to rescue them. How he wished he would have been able to help in the fight, but as he looked out the window to try and see what was going on, he saw his father being shot by the same French soldier who had killed his brother Henry, but it looked like he was only wounded as he was able to run away. Ebenezer hoped that he had made it to his friend Benoni Stebbins' house.

Sarah also heard the noise and prayed that her brothers David and Benjamin would be safe. Perhaps all would be well in the morning and she would awaken from the awful nightmare. But, sadly, it was not to be.

Chapter Five

*"Let the sighing of the prisoner
come before thee; according to the
greatness of thy power preserve thou
those that are appointed to die."*

Psalm 79:11

At first light, after hours of destruction, the captives, more than one hundred in number, were dragged out of the Meeting House by some of the French and Indian attackers and then marched outside the north gate of the palisade and across the snow-laden meadows outside of town. As they passed by her abandoned house, Sarah halted and looked longingly at it, realizing that perhaps never again would their family enjoy popping corn by the fire or making apple cider in the fall. She and her mother would never sing songs together as they worked on making quilts or spinning wool or making soap or candles.

Ebenezer shivered as he thought of his older brothers. Would he end up in the same place as they were? Were John and Zebediah still alive somewhere? Were they trying to make an escape? How he hoped that someday he would be reunited with them. Perhaps he could escape with them! He looked back to where his step-mother and baby sister Abigail were struggling to keep up and wished that he would be able to help carry the child, but his captor prodded him on. Besides that, he was burdened down with a heavy pack that his Indian master had forced him to carry and was straining to keep going himself.

Many of the attackers remained in the village continuing to fight the villagers who had survived and were holed up in the house Benoni Stebbins, Godfrey Nims' longtime friend who had been one of the three involved in the theft in Northampton, but was now, like Godfrey, a respected member of the community. Sarah's older brother David Hoyt, Jr.

was also in the fight. In the continuing battle, many Indians were wounded and killed. Perhaps the most significant casualty of the battle, as the captives were to learn later, was that Tsawenhohi, the "Great Chief" of the Huron Indians was mortally wounded.

The captives were marched over the Deerfield River about a mile to reach the foot of Mount Pocumtuck, a nearby mountain, where they rested. As she settled down on the cold, frozen ground, Sarah prayed that the survivors of the fight, perhaps her older David if he were alive, would somehow come and rescue them. She watched as her brother Jonathan and her childhood friend Ebenezer were the last in the line of captives who were struggling across the meadow and up the hill. They were both weighed down by their heavy packs, quilts tied and strapped to their foreheads, carrying plunder taken from their homes when the Indians ransacked them.

Soon after the fighting wore down in the village, militia from the neighboring towns arrived to help the survivors of the massacre. Sarah's hopes were ignited that with their arrival would come the answer to her prayers. These new men joined forces with the remaining survivors and began chasing the remaining attackers through the meadow. She watched the other captives silently praying that they would be rescued, but it was not to be. When their would-be rescuers sped towards them, they were met by an ambush by the French and Indian raiders who had gone ahead.

In the ensuing battle, nine villagers were killed and many more wounded. Much to her dismay, among those killed were her older brother, David, Jr. and Joseph's father David Alexander. All her hopes of rescue were dashed as she watched in horror as the remaining would-be rescuers retreated back to the village.

After the meadows fight, the despondent captives were led up the mountain and watched in dismay at the desolation of their town. Ebenezer counted about seventeen burning houses, one of which was his own. As he watched his home burning, he was overcome with grief and he knew in his heart that his precious little sisters lay dead in the ashes. He fell to his knees and hugged himself. Brushing tears from his eyes, he hoped that no one would condemn him if they saw him crying.

Never again would he hear Hittie, Mary and Mercy singing songs, or watch the three of them playing with their corn husk dolls or listen to them as they proudly recited their Bible verses that they had learned. It was all his fault they lie in ashes. If he hadn't put them in the cellar would they be alive with him now? He watched his dear step-mother as she cradled little Abigail, grieving the loss of her babies and Henry, and fearing the fate of her husband Godfrey who was probably killed in the fight in the village.

Even though additional forces arrived to help the town, the remaining defenders decided that further pursuit of the attackers was not feasible. They were afraid that the enemy would kill their captives if pursued. Those in the village that were mourning the losses of their dead and captured loved ones begged the militia to stay and try again to rescue the captives, but most of the men left Deerfield, leaving only a small garrison of soldiers to protect the town which had suffered the loss of 56 killed, including nine women and 25 children.

Seeing the more than one hundred of his captive family and neighbors, Ebenezer wondered how many would survive the ordeal. Did his father escape with his wounds? He wanted to trust that God would protect them all, but his heart cried out as he asked Him why He felt so far away. Why was He letting them suffer so much tragedy? He remembered the words of Reverend Williams and prayed that he might "have grace to glorify His name, whether in life or death." Still he wished that he could take some action that would help them to survive capture and return home.

The Indians prodded them to continue moving up the mountain and the captives took one last look at their burning village as they trudged along. Many of the French had moved on ahead, anxious to get back to New France leaving the captives in the charge of their Indian masters. The men were roped together and marched at the head of the line, leaving the women and children to drag behind. Most of the women were grieving for their murdered children. They continued on for miles through the snow, often stumbling in their grief and weakness.

Sarah watched as her brother Jonathan and friend Ebenezer struggled and fell many times with their heavy loads. She wanted to help them but when she motioned to her Indian master that she would like to help ease their burden, he angrily told her, "No!" She realized that they would be expected to carry the packs all the way to New France. She couldn't see her father, as he was up ahead of the line with the other men also carrying a heavy burden. She hoped that he wasn't suffering as much as Jonathan and Ebenezer were, as he was suffering from wounds he received when trying to fight off the attackers in their home.

After walking several miles through the deep snow, they stopped in a grove of spruce and the Indians told them to throw away their shoes and put on fur-lined moccasins made of deerskin. Sarah hated throwing away the beautiful shoes that Ebenezer had made for her before her life had so drastically changed, but she quickly put on the unfamiliar footwear.

Ebenezer and Jonathan removed their packs and rubbed their raw foreheads where their packs had been strapped. As it was growing dark, they looked around for shelter and realized that they would be sleeping on the ground with only the overhanging branches for shelter. The Indians cut branches for the women and children to sleep on, but made the men sleep on the cold wet snow. Sarah wrapped in her cloak trying to keep warm as the wind kicked up and constantly dropped melting snow on her. All around she could hear the mothers trying to comfort their crying children. She prayed and tried to comfort her mother and little sister Abigail who were shivering in the cold. She offered to hold her baby sister, but her dazed mother insisted on keeping the baby with her.

Trying in vain to sleep in the cold and wet with not even a fire for warmth, Sarah watched their captors drinking from ale that they had stolen from the town. In their drunken state they killed three-year old Marah Carter because she wouldn't stop her crying. Sarah watched her mother cover little Abigail's mouth with her cloak, to silence her before the captors also tried to kill her.

Sarah's betrothed Joseph saw their drunkenness as a chance to try and make an escape. He comforted his mother Mary as she mourned the death of his little sister Mary, and his father David, killed in the meadows fight. Creeping over to Sarah in the darkness, he whispered to her, "I make you a promise that I will come back for you and will bring others to help rescue the rest of the captives as soon as I am able. Take heart, my dear one and remain steadfast until I return. I give you my promise before God that I will come for you, no matter how long it takes," he whispered as he slipped away in the darkness.

After his escape, Sarah prayed for his safety and was finally able to fall asleep wrapped in her cloak, sleeping fitfully for a few hours on the cold ground.

In the morning the injured French Lieutenant de Rouville summoned Reverend Williams and told him that one of the captives had escaped. "Tell the English that if anyone else tries to escape, the rest of the prisoners will be burned," he warned.

Upon hearing this dreaded announcement that Joseph's escape had been discovered, Sarah's hopes were once more dashed and any hope of rescue fled. She hoped that he had made it back safely and was not re-captured or killed.

Later that morning Sarah's Indian captor unloaded his pack and made a pack from the quilt he had ripped from Sarah's bed, the one she had made for her wedding to Joseph. He placed some of his loot into the new pack and motioned for Sarah to pick it up. Her captor took it from her and placed it on her back and strapped it to her forehead with a leather cord. He gave her some moose jerky and told her to start walking.

Faint with hunger, she chewed on the tough jerky as they continued on their march. Soon they came to a river which moved so swiftly that it was not frozen over. The Indians carried the small children on their backs, but made the rest of the captives wade into the icy cold water. Sarah stepped into the thigh high river trying to hold onto her skirt to keep it from freezing, but as she did so her pack began to slip. She was afraid that she would lose her balance on the slippery rocks and be plunged into the raging river to meet an instant death, so she let down her skirt, which began to freeze to her legs which were now so numb she had no feeling in them.

Ebenezer watched as Sarah continued crossing the icy river, the wind whipping through her beautiful golden red hair that was loosely hanging down her back under the cord that held her pack. As she finally reached the other side of the river, he tried to reach down and help her up the steep bank, but his Indian master forbade him from assisting her.

Completely out of breath from the ordeal of crossing the icy river and with legs so cold and numb that they could hardly move, the captives finally made it to a clearing where the Indians had built a fire for them to dry their clothes and get warm, the first fire that they had had since being led away from the Meeting House.

Oh, how she wished she could be with Joseph, but she feared that he had not made it safely back to the town, since no rescue attempts had been made. As they rested by the fire, she watched as several Indians who had been at the rear of the column passed by with scalps hanging from their belts. She recognized the blonde scalp of her brother David and cried out for him. Seeing one that was dark like Joseph's she was at first terrified but then was relieved to see that it was too long and curly to be his. Clinging desperately to the promise he had made to her, she still had hope that one day they would be reunited and wed, but hopes were dimming as she witnessed more and more tragic deaths with no help in sight. Now her only goal was to survive the ordeal or to die quickly and join her loved ones in Heaven.

Ebenezer watched as the captors carried some of the children on their shoulders, including Reverend Williams' daughter Eunice. He had heard that the Indians desired children whom they could adopt into their families, especially young ones to whom they could teach Indian ways and customs. Ebenezer was worried when he saw that his stepmother was having a difficult time keeping up with the group because of the burden of carrying his little sister Abigail, and was relieved when one of the Indians took the child and carried her up the mountain.

As she sat on the cold ground resting from the crossing, Sarah kept her eye on the captors and saw when the last Indians who had been at the river crossing finally made it to the place where the remainder of them rested and waited for those who were carrying their wounded relatives.

She noticed that one whom she'd seen before carrying the severely wounded warrior, their "Great Chief," came up the hill much later than the others. He no longer carried the chief on his back and Sarah wondered if he had stayed behind to bury him near the river. Noticing his grief-stricken face, she also observed that it seemed to be a kind one. She saw for the first time that he was wearing a cross around his neck and she felt an odd sense of compassion for him as he struggled with grief for his dead chief.

She wished somehow that he would be her master instead of the cruel one that was now forcing her to leave the warmth of the fire before she had even begun to get warm or dry her clothes. He told her to pick up her pack and start up the snowy incline to the top of the hill where Reverend Williams was pacing nervously back and forth looking for his wife Eunice.

Reverend Williams' Abenaki master had forced him to be separated from his wife who, like Ebenezer's step-mother Mehitable, was having trouble keeping up with them. Upon reaching the top of the mountain he heard the exhausted Reverend Williams begging his master to let him go down the mountain to see why his wife had not yet arrived, but his master refused. The pastor asked each one of the captives passing by if they knew what had happened to his dear wife, who was still recovering from childbirth and had been struggling on the march.

"Oh, dear Reverend Williams, we are so sad to say that while trying to cross the river, she fell into it and one of the Indians slew her with his hatchet!" one of them cried.

Sarah remembered how earlier that day her pastor had been permitted to speak to his wife and help her walk. As they tread through the icy ground, his wife Eunice told him that her strength was failing and that he must expect for her to part from him.

"I pray that God will preserve your life and the life of our dear children," she had bravely told him. As he wept for her, he thanked God that she would now be free from the horrors ahead and be safe in Heaven where they would someday be reunited. He tried to comfort the rest of the captives while he struggled with his own sorrows.

They travelled up and down hilly terrain about twenty miles, plodding through about two feet of snow, made difficult by recent thawing. The captives had no snowshoes, making travel extremely strenuous. Many more of the weak were killed with swift blows from hatchets, including little Marah Carter's seven month old sister Hannah and ten year old Jemima Richards. Exhausted and spent, they stopped at the Green River before scaling another mountain.

Continuing along, another nursing baby and a young girl, too weak to make the march were also slain. Sarah prayed that her two year year old sister Abigail would not be next.

When they reached their camp for the night, Sarah heard one of the Indian masters talking to Reverend Williams' master and saying that they should kill and scalp him.

"Do you intend to kill me? Williams asked his master. "If so, then please let me know because my death will bring the guilt of blood upon you."

His master assured him that he wouldn't kill him. Sarah was relieved that her beloved pastor's life would be spared and began to hope that they would all survive this horrible trial.

Sarah and her family were with different Indians. The Indians believed that whichever of them touched a captive first would get to keep that captive. Sarah's father's master was an Eastern Indian, a Pennacock, who spoke some English, but her and Jonathan's master spoke very little, mostly grunting and pointing to make his commands known to them. Her mother and sister Abigail and brother Ebenezer were with another group of Indians.

Sarah watched as her mother struggled to carry her two-year old sister Abigail. As she kept lagging behind, Sarah was relieved when one of the Indians took Abigail in his arms and continued on. But when Abigail kept crying for her mother, Sarah watched in horror as he dashed her to the icy ground and slew her with a hatchet, then threw her down into a forty foot gorge. Her mother sank to the ground, gripping her sides and wailing for her baby girl. Her father turned to see what had happened and, though he was bound, tried to run back and comfort his grieving wife. His master jerked on the cord that held him and told him to keep going.

"She make too much noise," he admonished. "She alert pursuers where we are."

Shaking uncontrollably, Sarah realized that maybe they wouldn't survive this trial after all.

Chapter Six

*"I said in the cutting off of my days,
I shall go to the gates of the grave:
I am deprived of the residue of
my years. I said, I shall not see the
Lord, even the Lord in the land of
the living: I shall see man no more
among the inhabitants of the world.*

Isaiah 38:10-11

As they got ready for the night, some of the captives began to fear that the Indians were preparing to burn some of them as they had repeatedly threatened. Sarah wondered if any of the other captives had escaped as Joseph had, causing the Indians to kill them. Feeling a distressing uneasiness, she crept over to Ebenezer and shared her fears.

"Perhaps we should tell Reverend Williams that the Indians are peeling bark from several trees and it looks like they are going to build a huge fire," she told him.

"It doesn't look good. It's something that they have not done since we began our journey," he agreed.

When they told Reverend Williams their fears, he tried to encourage them. "Would the Indians have marched 300 miles to Deerfield in the middle of winter, risking death, starvation and injury and taking over a hundred captives back with them if they intended on killing us all now?" he reasoned. "Perhaps they plan on selling us to the French or back to the English for money," he continued. "However, they might want to adopt some of us into their families," he admitted, "but they can act nothing against us but as they were permitted by God, and I am persuaded that He will prevent such severities."

Momentarily reassured, Sarah was suddenly stricken to see her captor, the one the Indians called Gassisowangen take her brother Jonathan and bind him with strong leather cords. Gassisowangen was the nephew of Tsawenhohi, the "Great Chief" of the Hurons who had been wounded in the skirmish at the Stebbins house and later died and was buried by the kind Indian named Thaovenhosen.

Gassisowangen held on to Jonathan and shouted, "I demand that this captive be turned over to me to avenge the death of our chief!" According to the Mourning War tradition, the nephew, as the closest living relative of their chief, had the right to demand the slaughter of a captive as consolation to the grieving family.

Hardly breathing, Sarah listened to her master talking about putting her brother to the flames to be tortured. With shaking hands she searched through the Bible her father had given her before he was led away and, reading verses in the Psalms by the light of the flames, she cried out to the Lord,

> *"Mine eye is consumed because of grief; it waxeth old because of all mine enemies. Depart from me, all ye workers of iniquity; for the LORD hath heard the voice of my weeping. The LORD hath heard my supplication; the LORD will receive my prayer. Let all mine enemies be ashamed and sore vexed: let them return and be ashamed suddenly."*

She repeated these verses over and over to block the sound of the Indians as they gathered together arguing about Jonathan's fate.

The Indians were caught between their old Mourning War traditions and their loyalty to their Christian faith and Jesuit teachers. The younger warriors, including Gassisowangen, were demanding their rights as victors and wanted revenge.

Hearing a rustle behind her, Sarah turned and was horrified to see some of the young warriors begin peeling more bark off a tree in order to make a stake on which Jonathan was to be tortured and killed. Her worst fears were now happening and she could not bear any more grief.

"Oh, no, Lord! May it not be! They are going to kill him!" she cried. "Oh, Father, why have you forsaken us?"

Then she watched as the warrior Thaovenhosen slowly stood up to speak. She recognized him as the kind faced one who had carried the wounded Great Chief and then buried him by the river. He was not a chief and had no right to an opinion, but he boldly pleaded for the life of Jonathan. Although she didn't know at the time what he was saying, she learned later after she was familiar with the Huron language what he had said.

In the Huron tradition everyone had an equal right to speak their opinion before decisions were made.

"Fellow citizens of Lorette," he began, "let me remind you that we are Christians and dire cruelty is unbecoming to the Christian name." As his fellow warriors looked at him in surprise, he continued, "This injury cannot be branded upon the reputation of the Hurons of Lorette without the greatest disgrace."

Most of the younger Hurons didn't agree with him and pressed harder for their traditional rights.

"If we don't do this," one cried, "it will bring ruin to us all, for how can we let our Great Chief's death go unpunished when it will mean our enemies will grow more ferocious, and to become bolder to bring us harm!"

Seeing that appealing to Christian values was not succeeding, Thaovenhosen switched his argument to traditional Huron values, as he later told the captives. "I also am a relative of the Great Chief whose death we all mourn," he reminded them. "To me also a captive is due, and I contend that such is my right! I claim this one as my own!" Already speaking out of turn, he boldly continued, "If anyone lays hands on him against my will, let him look to me for chastisement!" The others in the assembly were shocked.

Gassisowangen glared at Thaovenhosen and cursed under his breath, "This is not over! We will see what our Great Chief's mother decides when we get back to our village!" No one else spoke, and the confrontation ended.

Jonathan was untied and released into the care of his new master Thaovenhosen. The warriors agreed that men would not be tortured and killed, but any women and children too weak to travel, would still be killed. Even though the present disaster was avoided, the terrors were far from over.

Relieved to see Jonathan released unharmed, Sarah ran to him and held him and wept. All she could do was to hold him and cry, "Oh, Lord, Oh Lord, Oh, Lord!"

The next morning Sarah witnessed another of her beloved neighbors, pregnant Waitstill Warner, killed because she was nearing the time of delivery of her baby and was too weak to travel. Waistill's husband broke down with heaving sobs as he grieved for little Sarah and Waitstill who were now left without their mother to bring them comfort through this terrible nightmare.

It was as the warrior council had agreed and Sarah determined that no matter what, she would do whatever she could do to survive and would help those who were in such deep distress. She gathered the Warner girls into her arms and held them while they sobbed for their mother.

"Do you think my mommy is in Heaven with our new baby brother or sister?" little Sarah asked.

"I know she is and she is looking down on you now and praying for your safety," Sarah assured her. After several minutes, she could hear the deep breathing of the little girls and hoped that when they awoke the next morning that they would be able to face the challenges that would most assuredly lie ahead.

They reached the frozen Connecticut River on that fourth day of their trek northward to New France. They found that the enemy had cached sleighs and provisions in a camp near the river. The captors built a fire and roasted some of the moose that they had stored there and all the captives ate hungrily, savoring each bite. Putting their wounded, the remainder of the loot they had taken from Deerfield, and several of the children on the sleighs which were pulled by dogs, the captors told them they must get up and keep going.

They continued their journey, travelling a great distance through ankle deep freezing water. Some of the men captives had to pull the sleighs in addition to carrying their heavy packs. Reverend Williams wasn't one of them. Perhaps the Indians wanted to keep up his strength so that he would draw more money when later ransomed because of his status in the colony.

On the fifth day, two grandmothers, Hepzibah Belding and Mary Frary were killed, too frail to even start the day. Twenty-nine year old Hannah Carter was also brutally slain. Sarah wanted to comfort her neighbors, but she was too distraught over the death of Abigail and Ebenezer and the near death of Jonathan and her separation from her parents to be of any help.

Shortly after that, Sarah watched in horror as Ebenezer Nims' step-mother Mehitable was slain.

Ebenezer wept for his step-mother who had raised him since he was just a few years old after his mother died. Never more would he hear her singing in the kitchen with his younger siblings or smell her wonderful apple fritters cooking or taste the delicious corn cakes she made with pure butter and maple syrup on top. Never would he be delighted with the beautiful quilts she made. He was devastated that his father would suffer even more grief and tragedy than he had already endured and he fervently prayed for the dear man who had now lost his second wife. He also prayed for his family that remained back in Deerfield, if any had survived, and he prayed for himself to be able to have the strength to keep going.

The sixth day of the march being the Sabbath, they rested, and Reverend Williams was allowed to pray and preach a sermon to the captives. He prayed for each of the dead captives and those who were slain in the massacre in Deerfield and reminded the captives that nothing happened or would happen that the Lord had not allowed. Sarah and the rest of the prisoners were somewhat encouraged as the pastor spoke from memory Lamentations 1:18:

> *"The Lord is righteous: for I have rebelled against his commandment: hear, I pray you, all people, and behold my sorrow: my virgins and my young men are gone into captivity."*

The pastor then admonished the captives to search their hearts and confess any sins they may have committed, so as not to hinder the Lord's hearing their prayers and blessing them.

When the pastor led the captives in singing Psalm 100, the one that his dear little sisters had shared with him what seemed like a lifetime ago, Ebenezer slipped away from the gathering. He sat under some spruce bows that were dripping large dollops of snow down his back and onto his head.

Ebenezer wasn't even aware of it as the wet snow mingled with tears of grief that he had been unable to shed until then.

Sarah followed him, and seeing him grieving, she reached out and took his hand and put her head on his shoulder. "We must be content to wait to see them in Heaven, and I fear that it may be soon," she whispered.

The next day, March 7th, a week after their capture, they marched on as usual, hungry and weak from lack of food. Always on the lookout for pursuers from the village, the Indians at the front of the procession were alarmed when they heard shots at the back of the line. Sarah, Jonathan and Ebenezer, and several other captives were bound while their masters went back to investigate the shooting.

As they sat tied to spruce trees on the cold ground, Sarah whispered to Ebenezer, "I hope it's Joseph keeping his promise that he would come back and rescue us." Ebenezer grunted and prayed that his father Godfrey was still alive and recovered from his wounds. He hoped that he would be among the rescuers, but he wasn't eager for his father to find out that his wife had been slain.

The captives waited in anticipation for several hours, hearing more shots in the distance. No one spoke as they were all listening for signs of rescue.

"I just know our rescuers are finally here!" Sarah excitedly repeated. "Joseph will save us!"

Ebenezer, however, had his doubts, but kept his thoughts to himself.

When the Indians reached the end of the line, they were happy to discover that some of their party who had been at the rear of the column had been shooting at a flock of geese that were flying overhead, trying to bring back some much needed food. Relieved that they were not being chased by the English, the Indians continued their shooting of the geese. The captives sat listening to the shots and hoping that it truly was their captives coming to rescue them, but were disappointed when they saw only their captors returning to the front of the line where they roasted the geese, feasting hungrily but sharing only small amounts with the captives. When the Indians had had their fill, they released the captives, continuing their treacherous journey northward, once more dashing Ebenezer's and Sarah's hopes of being rescued.

Cold and weary, the captives marched on day after day with a scarcity of food. Dodging wet branches flung in their faces by the person in front of them, they struggled to keep going. Sometimes they ate nothing but whatever roots they could find. As they trudged on through the bitter cold, more and more of the weak, mostly women and babies, were killed. Sarah was determined to persevere although she was afraid that her mother would not be able to endure the deprivation and loss.

After several days they came to a large river that branched off the Connecticut River. Sarah was distressed to see the captives scattered into smaller groups, each going separate ways. She watched in dismay as her mother, still weak and grieving the loss of her beloved children, was led up a mountain, disappearing into the heavy mist. She thought that this would be the last sight of her dear mother and clung to her father and wept. He, too, was distraught at the separation from his wife and the death of his children and was unable to comfort her.

Still racked with grief, her father was taken by his Pennacock master who told him that they would be going to their village in the mountains to the northeast. Before leaving Sarah, Deacon Hoyt quickly reached into his pocket and pulled out the precious family Bible now worn and wet from their punishing journey.

"Let this be a consolation to you, my Little Fox," he said. "Keep it with you always. You will find strength to endure in the precious words inside. Read it each day and remember wherever you are, know that I will always be with you and your mother and brothers and sisters in my heart. Should anything happen to me, we will surely meet again in Heaven someday. Remember to hold fast to your faith, Child," he said as he drew her close to his heart. "Take care of your brother and remember to pray for us all."

Grasping the treasured book, she watched in tears as her father and Jacob Hickson, a young garrison soldier, and Stephen Williams, son of her pastor Reverend Williams were led away. The Pennacocks split into several smaller groups looking for their family members who awaited them in the hunting territories in the mountains. Because her father and Hickson had fought the Pennacocks in earlier battles, they were treated like slaves. Since their masters had not had success while hunting, they didn't give Sarah's father and Jacob Hickson enough food to survive; they were left to scrounge whatever they could, and, as Sarah didn't learn until much later, the two men eventually starved to death in the cold mountains.

After her father's departure, they rested while the enemy's wounded recovered. Lieutenant Hertel de Rouville, also wounded, had ordered the time to renew their strength and heal from their wounds. Sarah's master gave her some more dried moose jerky from his pack. She shared it with Ebenezer and Jonathan. As she gazed into the small fire, she took out the Bible and tried to find a verse that would help. Since it was too dark to read by the firelight, she turned to the familiar twenty-third Psalm which she had memorized as a child:

"The Lord is my shepherd, I shall not want. He maketh me to rest in green pasture, and leadeth me by the still waters.

He restoreth my soul, and leadeth me in the paths of righteousness for his Name's sake. Yea, though I should walk through the valley of the shadow of death, I will fear no evil; for thou art with me: thy rod and thy staff, they comfort me.

Thou dost prepare a table before me in the sight of mine adversaries:

thou dost anoint mine head with oil, and my cup runneth over. Doubtless kindness and mercy shall follow me all the days of my life, and I shall remain a long season in the house of the Lord."

As she recalled the words of this beautiful Psalm, she tried to take courage as her father had encouraged her, but little did she know that before the day was out, she would need to draw on all the courage she could find.

Chapter Seven

"But he giveth strength unto him that fainteth, and unto him that hath no strength, he increaseth power.

Even the young men shall faint, and be weary, and the young men shall stumble and fall.

But they that wait upon the Lord, shall renew their strength: they shall lift up the wings, as the eagles: they shall run, and not be weary, and they shall walk and not faint."

Isaiah 40:29-31

A few days later Sarah and Ebenezer observed Reverend Williams so bruised and bloody from their grueling ordeal that he could only stand by hanging on to a tree. His master came to him and said that they must run that day. "I'm sorry, but even though I would like to obey you, I fear that I cannot!"

His master pointed his hatchet at him and said, "Then I must dash out your brain!"

"I suppose then you will do so and even take my scalp for I am not able to travel with speed," the pastor lamented.

Sarah and Ebenezer and Jonathan were afraid to lose their beloved leader and encourager and began to pray for God to spare his life. As soon as they ended their prayer, the pastor's master lowered his hatchet and forced Reverend Williams to keep going.

The pastor called out to the Lord to give them all strength to endure, and even though they didn't run that day, they were forced to travel as much distance as they usually did in two. Ebenezer offered to help Reverend Williams, but was not allowed to do so. He knew that any help for his pastor could only come from the Lord, so he prayed fervently for his safety.

As they marched, the wind blew harder and Sarah's hood kept falling back. Ebenezer gazed at her beautiful golden red hair and hoped that the Indian warriors wouldn't desire those stunning locks as a trophy. He didn't know how they decided whom to kill and whom to let live, but he vowed that he would do everything in his power, with God's help, to make sure she stayed alive. Even if she couldn't be his wife, he wanted her to survive and have a good life even if it were with Joseph instead of with him.

Before ascending another mountain, they stopped and the captives were finally given snowshoes. Sarah had to learn how to walk in them, but it did make it easier to travel; however she had to hitch up her partially frozen, soaked skirts in order to trudge through the slushy snow. Ebenezer was relieved to finally be able to trudge through the snow without having wet feet. His back and forehead continued to cause him pain as he struggled with the heavy pack up the steep terrain.

Ebenezer heard a small child crying, "I want my mommy!" He asked his new master Thaovenhosen if he could go comfort the little one who had lost her mother and try to keep her quiet. He was afraid that she would be killed as he had seen happen to the other young children who would not stop crying. Thaovenhosen nodded his assent, and Ebenezer crept over to the little girl. She immediately calmed down when he started to sing the last Psalm that he sang to Mary, Mercy, and Hittie. Sarah's heart was warmed to see how lovingly he cared for the little girl as he quietly wept for his little sisters that he would never see again.

Putting the child down in her quilt covered bed, he broke down in sobs. "Oh, Lord, why did I put them in that cellar?" he cried. "If only I had held them in my arms and protected them they might be here today and I could be singing songs with them and telling them stories to help them sleep. Now I only have little Abigail left and I don't even know who has her."

Sarah drifted off to sleep praying for Ebenezer and his broken heart.

After several days of difficult travel through the mountains, subsisting only on moose meat, ground nuts, cranberries and fish, the party reached Lake Champlain, the largest body of water Sarah and Ebenezer had ever seen. The Abenakis called it *Bitawbagok*. The frozen lake was very rough and uneven making travel almost impossible. Reverend Williams prayed to God to give them relief, and in answer to his prayers, God sent a few inches of snow to make it much softer on their frozen and bleeding feet.

Marching northward along the icy lake for several more days and after seven weeks of difficult travel, they finally reached Fort Chambly where the French and Indians had gathered before marching south for the attack on Deerfield. Some of the captives, including Reverend Williams were allowed to go with some of the French inhabitants of the fort to their homes.

Sarah, Jonathan, and Ebenezer were delighted when a French woman named Madame Charon entered their camp and invited them back to her home where she fed them warm freshly baked bread, the first they'd eaten since being captured, and other delicious food. Having eaten so very little on the march north, it was difficult for them all to mind their manners and not gobble down their meal. Thinking they would be sent back to the camp upon finishing their meal, they ate very slowly, savoring the warmth of the fire and the comfort of being treated kindly. They dried their moccasins, blankets, and stockings by the fire. Sarah was surprised when Madame Charon offered her a place to sleep on her couch while Jonathan and Ebenezer were given beds of straw near the fire.

Hoping that they could stay there until they were ransomed or rescued, they were all disappointed when in the morning a French soldier came to the house and took them back to the camp at Fort Chambly. The camp was in a state of uproar as the French and Indians argued over which captives would remain with the French and which would go with the Indians.

After intense negotiations, Lieutenant Hertel de Rouville took the French fur trader Jacques de Noyon who had married Sarah's friend Abigail Stebbins, Noyon's wife Abigail, and other members of the Stebbins family to New France in his custody. Having been on several other raids he and his men knew that his captives could be ransomed by French officials for payment, exchanged for French prisoners held by the English, or become settlers to increase the French population in New France.

Ebenezer hoped that his little sister, four year old Abigail, would be able to come with him, but he watched in despair as he saw her being carried away by her captor from the Iroquois of the Mountain tribe. Not understanding what was happening, she smiled and waved and said she would see him tomorrow. He never saw her again as she ended up being adopted by the tribe and remained in New France until she died.

Upon arriving in Canada, young Abigail Nims was under the care of the wife of the chief of the Iroquois of the Mountain. As were the Hurons, these Indians were Christians and treated little Abigail and a fellow prisoner a few years older than she named Josiah Rising very kindly. They were soon adopted into the tribe, given Indian names and soon after baptized by the priest at the Mission of Sault-au-Recollet as Catholics. She was given the name Marie Elisabeth Nims and Josiah was from then on called Ignace Raizenne. In 1715 when Abigail was fifteen and Josiah was twenty-one they were married. When attempts were made to redeem them many years later, they refused to leave their new home in New France and remained there until their deaths, many years later.

The remaining captives were taken by their Indian captors back to their respective home villages. The Hurons took Ebenezer, Sarah and Jonathan and set out for their village after a hasty breakfast of bread and venison.

From Fort Chambly, they continued eastward along a wide river, while the French travelled westward toward Montreal, or "Hochelaga" as the Huron captors called it, with the rest of the captives. They were only able to say a quick goodbye to their friends and neighbors. Reverend Williams admonished the three young people to keep their faith in the Lord, to remember their Catechism, and to obey God's commands to love their enemy as he joined the group heading west towards Montreal. They all promised their beloved pastor that they would do so.

As the small party walked through the wilderness, Ebenezer and Jonathan were given bows and arrows by their captors. Their masters had to teach them how to use them because the English rarely did any hunting except with their flintlock rifles.

"We will hunt for food in the forest," the Indians indicated as they stood and walked away from the fire where they had been warming themselves.

When Sarah stood to follow them, her captors stopped her. "You stay behind and guard the fire," they charged Sarah with gestures as they started out on their hunting expedition.

Ebenezer was worried about Sarah and was reluctant to leave her alone. They had been hearing wolves in the distance all day and he was afraid that she might encounter them while they were gone and be defenseless against their attack.

"Do you know how to use a firearm?" he asked as he handed her one of the muskets that the Indians had taken from his house. He quickly showed her how to use it as the Indians waited impatiently for him to join them. They only had a few hours of daylight left to bring back food if they were to have anything to eat that night. He prayed that she would be able to defend herself should the wolves come near her.

The Indians indicated that she would be safe as long as she stayed near the fire and kept it going.

Sarah watched as they left her alone and disappeared like ghosts into the forest. She sat rigidly against a spruce tree, hugging her frozen knees, listening to every sound that whispered through the trees, and watching every shadow that crept in the darkness as she carefully attended the fire.

She had often watched her father shooting turkeys, ducks, geese and deer in the meadow but had never in her life tried to shoot a musket. She hoped she would be able to use the firearm if any of those dreadful wolves or other predators came near. She tried holding the musket to see how it felt, but it was awkward and cumbersome in her small hands. Setting it back down close to her, she prayed that she wouldn't have to use it.

She pulled out her Bible and tried to find courage and holding it close to the light of the fire, found a verse that her father had read to her when she was afraid of the dark as a child. It was Isaiah 41:10:

> *"Fear thou not, for I am with thee: be not afraid, for I am thy God: I will strengthen thee, and help thee, and will sustain thee with the right hand of my justice."*

After the men had been gone a few hours, Sarah heard a rustling in the woods behind her. Thinking it was the men returning she hailed them. "Did you find any game?" she haltingly called out, hoping that it was really them and nothing more threatening. When there was no response, she turned again towards the rustling sound and looked up into the yellow eyes of an angry, gray wolf. As she repeated the verse from Isaiah with a pounding heart, she bent over and slowly reached for the flintlock and with shaking hands wet with perspiration, shot the creature in the head. Not being able to look at the fierce eyes of the slain animal, she kicked it away into the darkness.

Deep in the forest, Ebenezer spotted a rabbit and quickly put the arrow in his bow as his captor had shown him, but even though his master stood behind him trying to help guide him, in his excitement he missed his target and the rabbit scampered away. He was ashamed that he missed the opportunity to provide much needed food and had let down Sarah, Jonathan, and also the Indian captors. He vowed he would learn to use the bow and arrow so that he would not be humiliated again.

As it was getting dark, they headed back to the camp. Making their way through the woods, they heard a single shot from the flintlock. Rushing back to see what had happened, they found Sarah rocking back and forth on her feet and staring blankly into the fire beside the bloodied wolf.

That night they ate the wolf, the only food they had eaten since leaving Fort Chambly days before.

Early the next morning they continued on their journey for several hours. Again the men went into the woods and left Sarah behind. After trudging several miles up and down hills in the wilderness they spotted a small deer. Ebenezer's master

Gassisowangen shot the animal and after skinning and gutting it, he gave the skin to Jonathan to carry and put the deer carcass on Ebenezer's shoulders where he carried it all the way back to camp. Ebenezer felt that this was his punishment for missing the rabbit the day before. He was more determined than ever to master the art of shooting.

When Sarah heard them thrashing through the woods, she feared another wolf encounter and once more reached for the flintlock. Hands shaking, she pointed it towards the sound and was relieved to see the Indian masters followed by Jonathan. Several minutes later Ebenezer appeared, exhausted and covered with dried blood from the deer hanging from his shoulders. They cooked some of the meat for their dinner and smoked the rest to eat on their journey.

The next day they came to a small river and the way was much easier as the surrounding land was flat. They were allowed to stop along the river and break open the ice to splash water on their faces and take drinks of the refreshing cold water using their hands as cups. It tasted so good after so many weeks of drinking melted snow along the trail. Ebenezer washed off the blood from the deer carcass as best he could using dried leaves as a washing cloth.

After several days of travel, the large river, the St. Lawrence, was by now mostly free of ice. The Indians picked up some dugout canoes about forty or fifty feet long that they had stashed on the way south. They loaded their packs and the three captives and travelled northeast toward Quebec. How wonderful it was to sit in the bottom of the dugout and rest their weary legs and feet! Her feet were so bloody and swollen that Sarah didn't think she'd ever be able to wear beautiful shoes like the ones Ebenezer had made for her again.

Passing fields and French farms just now turning green with spring brought hope that their long winter would soon be over and that people from Deerfield would soon be able to come and rescue them. Ebenezer noticed how beautiful the farms were and regretted that he may never again be able to help his father work their farm or help his brothers tend the cows in the pasture where they had been seized all those months ago. Perhaps he would see John and Zebediah in Quebec when they reached that city.

Ebenezer and Jonathan were made to help paddle the canoes as they made their way through the deep waters, still laden with large chunks of ice in places. As they glided through the wide river, Sarah mourned for her brothers and sister who had been killed and prayed that her mother and father were safe and well. She thought of the more than a dozen captives who had died on the march and the dozens more that had been killed in the village.

She let her mind dwell on Joseph and dreamed that he would come to her rescue and take her home to be his wife as he had promised. Ebenezer sat behind Sarah in the canoe and watched her closely, as he also mourned his dead family and prayed for those left behind. He wanted to take Sarah in his arms and comfort her, but was again disheartened with the realization that the girl he had loved and been too shy to court until it was too late would never be his. He hoped, for her sake, that her intended husband had made it back safely to the village when he escaped captivity that first night of their march and would be able to arrange for their rescue. In the meantime, he would protect his friend and comfort her as best he could in the days ahead.

After several days of travel on the river, and thinking that Quebec was their destination, the three captives were surprised when they left the river before reaching that great city once known by the Indians as "*Stadacona,*" the capital of New France, and again headed overland. After walking about eight miles through the forest, travelling up a slight hill, they heard a great roaring sound that must have been coming from a huge waterfall. The Indians let out several loud whoops as they celebrated their coming to their village. The captives were greeted with a sight of a huge building with a cross on top, "*Notre Dame de la Jeune Lorette,*" Our Lady of the New Lorette, surrounded by several Indian longhouses and a few wigwams. They had reached the village of Lorette.

Chapter Eight

— ✑ —

"Hear my prayer, O Lord, and hearken unto my supplication: answer me in thy truth, and in thy righteousness.

And enter not into judgment with thy servant: for in thy sight shall none that liveth, be justified.

For the enemy hath persecuted my soul: he hath smitten my life down to the earth: he hath laid me in the darkness, as they that have been dead long ago:

And my spirit was in perplexity in me, and mine heart within me was amazed."

Psalms 143: 1-4

Soon a crowd of women and children came running to welcome their husbands, fathers and other warriors home after the several months of separation. They had feared that none would survive the bold attack and were delighted when they saw how many had returned. After their initial relief at seeing their loved ones safely returned, they began asking about their great chief. Soon their celebrations turned to wailing.

As soon as they saw the change in behavior of the Indians, the three captives feared what fate was in store for them. Would they still face the possibility of being tortured and killed by others of the chief's relatives or would they be adopted as children into the community? They had heard about the fearsome practice that the Indians had of making them run through the gauntlet where they would be forced to run between two lines of Indians who would kick and club them and push them to the ground. They hoped that they wouldn't have to endure such an ordeal, but feared that it would be so.

Soon their master Thaovenhosen led them to the door of one of the longhouses and motioned for them to go inside. It was hard to see in the dark, smoky interior, but eventually their eyes became accustomed to the gloominess inside. Hanging from the high beams of the longhouse were animal furs, dried plants, and baskets. Looking more closely in the darkness, they saw an old woman with dried leathery skin reclining on a platform of cut spruce branches covered in deerskin and furs. She was wrapped in beaver furs and her face showed no emotion.

"She will be the one to decide whether you are to be adopted or tortured and killed for revenge for killing our Great Chief," Thaovenhosen explained. "She is the mother of our Great Chief and my grandmother," he went on. Sarah was surprised that the decision of how they were to be treated was left up to a woman to determine. In their Puritan culture, only the men were charged with making such decisions.

Thaovenhosen and his grandmother talked for what seemed like hours while the captives remained standing in fear. Ebenezer reached for Sarah's shaking hand and she looked up to him with gratitude. She couldn't face the possibility of losing Jonathan now that he was all she had left of her family and Ebenezer, who was the only other person from home.

Hungry and tired, they continued to watch as the two Indians discussed their fate. Finally Thaovenhosen walked over to Jonathan and Ebenezer and motioned for them to come to his longhouse where they would sleep for the night. Sarah was to remain in the care of his stone-faced grandmother, Ashutaa, the most respected elder in the tribe. In the morning the tribe would assemble and in a formal ceremony after each member had his say, the fate of the three captives would be announced.

After a fitful night's sleep in the smoky longhouses the three captives were awakened by the sound of beating drums.

They heard the rustle of bodies moving to gather in a large clearing where they were taken for the ceremony.

Jonathan's original captor Gassisowangen, the one who had wanted to torture and kill him, spoke up first and again pled his case that he be allowed to kill and scalp him as revenge for the death of their Great Chief Tsawenhohi. Several others of the warriors also shouted for revenge, but Ashutaa silenced them and asked Thaovenhosen to speak up for Jonathan.

Sarah, again gripped by fear and holding on to the hands of Jonathan and Ebenezer, prayed for Thaovenhosen to prevail. After many anxious moments, they watched as Ashutaa granted him his request to take Jonathan as his adopted son.

Ebenezer, however, faced a different fate. Sarah watched nervously as some of the Indians broke into two long lines and some started beating on drums. The drums got louder and the beat grew faster and faster. Her heart echoed the beat. The rest of the Indians whooped and danced to the pulsing rhythm of the drums. The women waved the scalps that had been taken during the raid and march to New France. Sarah choked as she again saw her brother David's scalp and then couldn't believe it when she also recognized her brother Ebenezer's and baby sister Abigail's scalps. How could these savages take scalps of children? She was further dismayed to see the Indian children clapping hands and joining in the fray. Never again would she see her own little brother and sister clapping and singing. She felt her stomach churning and feared she would be sick, but ended up with dry heaves because of the lack of food she had eaten for the last several days.

Looking back to where the gauntlet was being set up, Sarah looked away as they stripped Ebenezer's clothes off and put a loincloth made of deerskin, two small squares one in front and one in back tied with a cord. He was pushed into the center of the lines and prodded with a spear by Gassisowangen, the Great Chief's nephew, who had wanted to have him burned on the march northward and had vowed to avenge the Great Chief's death. She couldn't take her eyes away as she watched Ebenezer being kicked and hit with clubs and pushed to the ground by the Indians who were seeking revenge. She was surprised to see that he made it through the gauntlet alive, though bloody and bruised.

Ebenezer looked up to Sarah with such passion in his eyes, like he was ashamed for her having to witness such a humiliating event. Sarah put her hand on her heart and watched as he was taken by Gassisowangen, who was now his master, to the longhouse. Since he survived the running of the gauntlet would he be adopted as a son like Jonathan or would he forever be a slave?

Ashutaa announced that she would keep Sarah to help her in her daily tasks and to help assuage her grief over the loss of her dear son Tsawenhohi, the former chief whose name meant, "the man who sees clearly" or "the hawk," as she told Sarah later. She instructed some of the women to take her to the river where she was told to bathe and take off her dirty clothes. Sarah was reluctant to shed all of her garments in front of the women, but upon seeing her hesitancy, they motioned for her to go behind a bush where she could have some privacy.

They gave her a tunic made of deerskin and embroidered with feathers and glass beads which had come in trade from Europe and which were painted with brightly colored designs. After struggling for over a month with her heavy skirt weighed down with mud and ice and snow, it was a pleasure to wear something so warm and soft and dry. Then they motioned for her to put on new moccasins to replace the filthy ones that she had worn for the entire journey to Lorette. After braiding her wet hair and placing a feather through the strands, they told her to follow them back to the longhouse where they made her burn her clothes in the fire that seemed to burn constantly, creating heavy smoke that made Sarah choke. The women wanted her to throw her Bible into the fire and take one of theirs which had been given to them by the Jesuit priest but she clutched it to her heart and adamantly refused to hand it over to them.

She spent the rest of the day learning how to grind corn to cook for the evening meal. Some of the women spoke a little English that they had learned from other captives and explained to her that she would need to go into the fields with them the next day to dig the ground for planting this year's crops of corn, squash, beans, and other food for the village.

The next morning on the way to the fields, Sarah saw a man wearing a long, black robe with a cord tied around his waist approaching. A large cross made of silver hung from his neck and he carried a book in his hands.

"My name is Father Louis D' Avaugour and I am the priest of this mission," he said. "I have brought you a Bible in English, which you may use."

"No, thank you," Sarah replied. "I have my own Bible that I brought with me from home. It has been in our family for many generations and was given to me by my father before he was taken away on the journey here."

"I will permit you to keep it; however, you will be required to attend our Mass in the morning with the rest of the captives."

When she said that she did not want to worship God in a Catholic church, Father D' Avaugour laughed and said, "Perhaps you have been sent by God to learn the true way to worship."

"I believe ours is the right way to worship," she argued.

Father D' Avaugour chuckled and said, "I believe that you will see that ours is the right way when you read your own Bible."

Sarah hardly believed that that would ever happen.

Father D' Avaugour then left her to talk to Jonathan and Ebenezer. When Sarah joined her friend and brother, they were wearing a combination of European cloth garments and deerskin leggings. Their hair had been shaved in the strange way of the Hurons with tufts of hair sticking out on top and all the way down to their necklines. On their feet were new moccasins like Sarah's.

"Did they try to persuade you to become converts to the Catholic faith?" Sarah asked.

"Oh, yes, but we told them that we would only worship God in the way we have been taught," Jonathan answered.

"We must obey the charge that Reverend Williams gave to us when we were separated from the rest of the captives," Ebenezer agreed.

The Indians treated Jonathan better than the other two because of his status as the captive who was saved from death by Thaovenhosen who had great authority in the tribe. Although his master was kind to Jonathan, it was hard for all three of the captives not to fear him because he was proud of the wounds he received from fighting their family, friends, and neighbors and often displayed them to the other Hurons.

And so they continued on with their daily life in Lorette.

While the men mostly spent their time away from the village hunting, fishing and trapping, Sarah worked with the other women planting, harvesting, grinding corn, making clothing from the animal skins that the men brought them, picking berries and maidenhair ferns, watching children and tending the fires in the longhouse.

Ebenezer remembered his vow to learn how to use a bow and arrow and asked his master to teach him. He practiced with the other young men in the village until he was skilled enough to go hunting with the men. He learned how to trap beaver for furs to trade with the French in Quebec. He and Jonathan also learned how to make dams in the streams surrounding their village where they would spear the fish that became trapped there. The two boys also learned how to make canoes for travel on the nearby rivers.

When he wasn't practicing his skills with the bow and arrow or out trapping, fishing, or hunting with the other men, Ebenezer learned how to make moccasins and snow-shoes like the ones they used on their journey to Lorette. It was certainly different from what he was used to when he would make shoes for the townspeople of Deerfield. One day as he sat making another pair of snowshoes, he remembered the beautiful shoes that he had made for Sarah before all the events that happened and changed his life. He vowed that one day he could return to Deerfield and make her a new pair to replace the ones that the Indians forced her to throw away after the attack on their village.

Ebenezer and Jonathan would often take turns and go to the docks in Quebec with their masters Thaovenhosen and Gassisowangen to sell vegetables and furs to the merchants and citizens of the town. Often their masters would leave them for short periods of time while they bartered furs with the merchants. While Ebenezer was there, he struck up a friendship with a young man named Samuel and another Ebenezer whose last name was Hill, and some of the other English men who had been captured from Wells, Massachusetts, in the previous war. Whenever he could sneak away from his master, he would meet with them and try to make plans for escape, but there were few opportunities for such meetings and when they did occur, they were often cut short when Gassisowangen would return from his trade with the merchants.

The first winter, about a year after they were captured, Thaovenhosen and Gassisowangen told them to put on their snowshoes and carry some large copper buckets to the forest.

"What are we going to do with these buckets?" Jonathan asked.

"Are we going to gather ice from the river?" Ebenezer added.

"You will see," Gassisowangen answered in Huron, which by now the two young men were able to understand. They could not speak it well yet, for they were unable to make some of the difficult sounds of the language, but at least they could understand much of it. They were also quickly learning to speak French as all of the Hurons of Lorette did.

They stopped by a stream and began to break up the ice to put into their buckets, but Thaovenhosen stopped them and told the two to gather several stones to carry to their destination.

Still not understanding what they were going to do with the stones, Ebenezer and Jonathan picked up enough stones from the partially frozen stream and put them in their buckets.

"Why do you think we are gathering stones?" Jonathan asked Ebenezer. "It doesn't make sense to me."

"I don't know," Ebenezer answered, "but I guess we'll soon find out."

Gassisowangen and Thaovenhosen then started walking deeper into the forest where they stopped at a grove of maple trees.

"We will make sugar today," Thaovenhosen explained.

Jonathan and Ebenezer were astonished. "Sugar? From trees?" they both exclaimed.

"How did you learn that you could get sugar from maple trees?" Ebenezer asked.

"We learned about it from Hum-isha-ma, the Iroquois woman. She told us that one day her father returned from a hunt and smelled something sweet coming from the kettle where her mother was boiling meat. She had found a broken maple limb and collected the sap from it and put it in the kettle with the meat," Thaovenhosen explained. When they tasted it and saw that it was good, they found a way to gather more sap and began to make sweet liquid.

"How will we get the sap from the tree?" Jonathan asked.

"You will see," his master explained.

Thaovenhosen told the boys to take their hatchets and hollow out a log. When they were finished, he cut a slash in a tree with his hatchet and the sap started to drip out into the chutes made from the hollowed out logs. They continued this process throughout the day and tapped several trees. They returned the next day to check on the sap and Thaovenhosen told them to build a fire. Then Gassisowangen told them to pick up the stones they had gathered from the stream the previous day and place them into the fire and wait until they were white hot. When the stones were hot enough he told the boys to retrieve them by using a ladle he had carried. Next he told them to place the hot stones into the hollowed out logs to make the sap boil. At first the sap turned to syrup. It took a lot of sap to make a small amount of the sweet liquid. The men told the boys to gather some into their buckets, but then after heating for quite a while, the syrup turned to crystallized sugar which could be stored without spoiling.

"We have heard about this maple sugar back in our village," Ebenezer said, "but I guess I never thought about how it was made. Most of our sugar comes from sugar cane from Barbados on the ships that land in Boston. It would be good if the people in our village could make sugar like this and we wouldn't have to purchase it from the traders."

Thaovenhosen just nodded and they gathered the sugar into the big kettles to bring back to the village.

"We will come back many times to do this," Thaovenhosen explained. The French like to trade the sugar with us so they can make their pastries and other delicacies that they enjoy eating. The traders like to take sugar cakes with them when they travel. They bring us beads from across the great waters that we use for our clothing and other items that we need."

Chapter Nine

"Then the Lord thy God will cause thy captives to return, and have compassion upon thee, and will return, to gather thee out of all the people where the Lord thy God hath scattered thee."

Deuteronomy 30:3

Ensign John Sheldon, local official and government agent had suffered greatly in the raid on Deerfield. His wife Hannah had been killed in the village along with several others of his family. His daughter Mary, daughter-in-law Hannah, and daughter Remembrance were all captured and carried off with the other captives to New France. In December of 1704 he and John Wells, who had also lost his wife in the raid, travelled to Boston to seek permission from authorities there to go to New France and try to recover some of the captives. Wells was trying to rescue his mother-in-law.

The Massachusetts Council granted them permission and chose two French prisoners to exchange and to guide them overland to Quebec. Governor Dudley, however, favored a different approach. He wanted to develop ties with New York in order to provide easier contacts with officials in New France. He contacted an Albany merchant named Captain John Livingston who had already established contacts in New France who agreed to lead the two Deerfield men there by an easier route from Albany to the Saint Lawrence River. The Massachusetts Council agreed with this approach and Sheldon and Wells set out in the company of Livingston from Albany along the well-used route along the Hudson River to Lake Champlain, and then the Richelieu River, the same way the captives had traveled a year before. At the mouth of that river, they then travelled the St. Lawrence to Quebec, arriving there in February 1705, a year after the Deerfield raid.

The men met with Canadian Governor Vaudreuil and handed him letters from the authorities in Boston which indicated that Massachusetts held about 150 French prisoners that they would be willing to trade for the English captives held in New France.

Governor Vaudreuil agreed and Sheldon and Wells were encouraged.

"However, before I will agree to release any English prisoners, you must agree to return 16 French prisoners who your colony has sent to the West Indies and England.

Sheldon and Wells didn't think that would be a problem, but knew that they would have to get permission from the Massachusetts Council before they agreed. Thinking that the Council would agree, they began to have hope that their mission would be a success and that all the captives would soon be released, but the feeling of hope and confidence was short-lived.

"I have one other stipulation," the governor continued. "You must also release the French privateer Pierre Maisonnat."

"Do you mean Captain Baptiste? But he is a pirate who captured several of our fishing vessels before Queen Anne's war even broke out!" Sheldon and Wells objected. "We cannot possibly agree to those terms!"

"Nonsense!" Captain Baptiste was only defending French territorial waters as he had a right to do. I insist that unless he is included in the exchange, none of your captives will be released!" Vaudreuil exploded.

"But he attacked and plundered several of our merchant ships even before Queen Anne's War broke. In addition, he captured several of our fishing vessels. Our government does not recognize your claim to those waters for fishing. We cannot accept those terms without further discussion with the authorities in Massachusetts," Sheldon protested. "I don't think that they will agree to such outrageous demands!"

"Be that as it may, those are my terms," Vaudreuil repeated.

Discouraged at this impossible turn of events, Wells spoke up, "Will you at least allow us to visit some of the captives before we depart?"

"That can be arranged," the governor conceded, "but remember my terms!" With that he ushered the two men out of the room.

While they stayed in Quebec learning of the locations of the captives, Ensign Sheldon received a letter from his daughter-in-law Hannah who was living with the French in Montreal. The men immediately set out to try and see her.

While Wells and Sheldon were in Montreal they were allowed to see Reverend John Williams who was staying with the Jesuit missionaries there.

"Oh, my dear friends! It is so good to see you!" the pastor tearfully exclaimed as he welcomed them into his small sleeping room. They were happy to see that their pastor seemed to be treated well. He even had a feather bed! He offered them bread, cheese, and fruit as they gathered around a small table he used as a writing desk. He had been writing in a journal each day recording his experiences of the raid, the march, and his captivity.

"Do you have news from home for me? Have you seen any of the others from our village?" Williams asked.

"We do have news," Wells said. "But could you first tell us if you have heard about where my mother-in-law might be?"

"Oh, my dear son," the pastor lamented. "That dear woman was one of those who were killed on the march north. She, along with my dear wife Eunice, is with our blessed Lord now and at peace. Our captors killed several of our women and some of the children who were too weak to travel." He went on to give them the names of those who had perished on the march.

Wells nodded and whispered, "Perhaps it is better this way so they don't have to endure the hardships of being held captive."

"That is true. Our Lord is sovereign," Williams acknowledged and then went on to tell the men of the fate of all those taken captive. Sheldon and Wells then told the news of all their family and neighbors from home as they continued eating the meal with the pastor.

"I received a letter from my daughter-in-law Hannah while we were in Quebec where she shared that all three of my children are alive. One is with the French and two are still with their Indian captives," Sheldon shared. "We are trying to make arrangements for their release, but we have run into some outrageous demands by Governor Vaudreuil." He related the Governor's demand for the pirate Baptiste and others.

"It will be difficult to obtain the release of the two held captive by the Indians," Williams explained. The French say that they have no influence over the Indians who are not subject to them. The Indians have adopted them into their families and refuse to let them go. We might have better success with those who are being held by the French, who are more willing to do exchanges for political and economic reasons."

"Or for the release of criminals like Baptiste," Sheldon lamented.

"I have tried to see my daughter Eunice, but the priests and Indians at Kahnawake will not allow me to talk to her," Williams went on. "They tell me that she does not want to see me and that she has been baptized into the Catholic faith and wants to remain with her Indian family. My heart is broken for her and I can't accept that she does not want to see me!" he said with such sorrow that the men turned away while the pastor wiped tears from his eyes. "I pray that you will be able to see your own dear children, Ensign Sheldon," he said with a broken voice.

"We will do our very best to see that all of our dear ones are brought home safely," he replied. "We only wish that the French would be more reasonable in their demands."

"Much as we had hoped, we are unable to secure your release at this time, Reverend Williams," Wells explained. "However, we must tell you that your wife's relatives, the Reverends Increase and Cotton Mather are making strenuous efforts to accomplish an exchange on your behalf. Governor Dudley is also working to do a prisoner exchange that will allow you all to be released. After we met with Governor Vaudreuil and he made those difficult terms, we sent Governor Dudley a letter explaining Vaudreuil's conditions for an exchange. In the meantime we are going to see if we can secure the release of some of the captives while we are here in New France. We will meet with some of the other officials while we are here and see what we can accomplish on your behalf."

Reverend Williams thanked them for their efforts and led them in prayer before they set out to try and visit some of the captives. The men were able to see a few of their Deerfield neighbors and word spread among the captives held in the various locations that rescue attempts were being made on their behalf.

When they heard the rumors, Sarah, Jonathan, and Ebenezer began to hope that perhaps they would soon be released.

After several months, Wells approached Canadian officials and was able to arrange for the release of Hannah, his son Ebenezer, the pastor's daughter Esther Williams, and two other captives who were living with the French. Governor Vaudreuil, for reasons unknown to the Deerfield men, agreed to their release and in May sent them back with an escort of six soldiers before receiving Governor Dudley's response to his demands.

Reverend Williams was able to send a letter to the captives who had been released with Sheldon and Wells before they left on their voyage from Quebec to Boston. In the letter he expressed his dismay that he would not be permitted to return with them or even to come and see them before their voyage. He prayed for God to guide them in His mercy and asked them to pray for him and the other captives that were left behind. He said that even though they would face more *"fiery trials,"* he asked them to pray that they could all be witnesses for God, to serve him, to keep the faith and with God's grace to *"suffer according to His will."* He reminded them that *"through much tribulation we must enter into the Kingdom of Heaven."*

Concerned that they might be tempted to look forward only to seeing their friends and family, to recover their lost property and possessions, and continue on with their life as they did previously, he counseled them *"with all freedom to glorify God in bringing forth much fruit."*

He urged them to read Luke 8:39:

> **"Return into thine own house, and show what great things God hath done to thee. So he went his way, and preached throughout all the city, what great things Jesus had done unto him."**

He told them that by doing that they would be complying with the revealed will of God, and reminded them of God's word in Psalm 50:15 that said,

> *"And call upon me in the day of trouble: so will I deliver thee, and thou shalt glorify me."*

What the Deerfield men didn't know was that the French governor also sent a personal envoy, Captain Augustin Legardeur de Tilly, Sieur de Courtemanche with them to supposedly facilitate the exchange of prisoners. This man's brother Charles Legardeur de Croiselle had been one of the soldiers at the Deerfield raid. The Captain's instructions were to gather intelligence while in Boston that they could use in further negotiations or raids on the English.

Chapter Ten

⁓

"And when they had brought them out, the Angel said, 'Escape for thy life: look not behind thee, neither tarry thou in all the plain: escape into the mountain, lest thou be destroyed'.

"Genesis 19:7

Frustrated with the failure of the Deerfield men to obtain their release, four of the captives decided to try to make an escape. Joseph Petty, who was living with a French family in Montreal, approached John Nims, Ebenezer's older brother who had been captured in October before the Deerfield raid. The two men made plans for their escape and in May during the Feast of the Holy Sacrament where the captives were allowed to roam free about the town, they met up with Martin Kellogg and Thomas Baker who had already tried unsuccessfully to escape. There the four men secretly laid their plans.

"You three meet me at my place in three days," Perry suggested. "I will gather guns and food for our escape."

"How will we know how to find you?" Nims asked.

"I will leave a sign by the river indicating the place where I live," he said.

The men agreed and made their way back to their dwellings. Three days later before the sun came up the four men met and paddled across the St. Lawrence River before the sun rose. There they abandoned the canoe and went overland to the south. Two days later they reached the Richelieu River nine miles south of Fort Chambly. They camped there and fashioned a crude raft and crossed the river, travelling south along the river bank.

After a week they arrived at Lake Champlain, but had no way to cross it.

"Let us pray to God that He would send us a way across," John Nims entreated. The others agreed and the men stopped to ask the Lord for provision. As they continued to walk south along the bank they found two abandoned canoes and thanked God for his answer to their prayer.

They took just one of the canoes and paddled down the east side of the lake. After several days of travelling like that, the wind kicked up to such an extent that they were forced to abandon the canoe and go by foot where they soon came to the Winooski River. They climbed upwards along this river until they came to the Green Mountains. Crossing the mountains, they reached the White River and had to stop and hunt for food as all their provisions were exhausted after having to travel overland during the heavy winds on Lake Champlain. The only food they were able to get was a few fish and some reptiles which they ate with thanksgiving. After resting for a few days, they continued on their journey by foot. Eventually they made it to the confluence of the White and the more familiar Connecticut River and built another crude raft which took them down the river towards their village.

After almost a month of difficult travel the four starved and exhausted men finally arrived back home where they were greeted with joy and thanksgiving by the residents.

As John saw the destruction of the village for the first time he was hoping that some of his family had survived. When he spotted his brother-in-law Benjamin Munn, his sister Thankful's husband, he asked,

"Is my father Godfrey and the rest of our family anywhere? Our house is nothing but ashes. Did any survive?"

"I wish I had better news for you, John. Your father was wounded and died a few weeks after the massacre," Munn answered. "Your three sisters, Mary, Mercy and little Hittie died in the fire where they were hiding in the cellar. Your sister Rebecca and her husband Phillip were killed and so was your brother Henry. Thankful and I hid in the underground shelter that was hidden by a snow bank so we survived. Your brother Ebenezer, your sister Abigail and your stepmother were captured and we do not know their fates."

"We must find a way to bring them home then!" he vowed as he wiped tears from his eyes.

"Do you know what happened to your step-brother Zebediah who was captured with you?" asked Benjamin.

"Zebediah took ill and died in captivity," John said. "He was ill for quite awhile and died peacefully, never losing his faith in God."

"I am so sorry to hear that. His sister Elizabeth was captured during the raid. I know that you two were very close. Let us continue to pray that she will be safe and return home," Benjamin said, trying to offer his sympathy.

After several minutes of silence, Benjamin continued. "We have heard that the Canadian authorities are demanding the release of the Pirate Baptiste before any captives will be allowed to return home."

"Yes, we heard that and that's why we decided to try and make our escape," John confirmed.

"In addition to that, the merchants and traders and sailors in Boston are adamant that Baptiste not be released because they fear the danger that would come to them if he were to be set free," Munn continued. "Governor Dudley is in favor of the pirate's release if the Canadian officials will assure him that all the captives, including those held by the Indians will be freed. The rumors are that once all the captives are returned that we will make an all out effort to re-capture this dreaded miscreant who will most likely continue to terrorize our naval forces and merchants."

"Word is that the governor was heard making an out-burst at the last meeting of the Massachusetts Council. *'We should hang the blackguard as an example to all the other pirates who would dare attack our merchant ships and then throw his sorry body into the deepest waters of the ocean to be devoured by the sharks!'*" Munn mimicked.

John laughed. "He must have been livid to make such a declaration!"

"Seriously though, we recently received word that the governor was proposing a formal treaty to make such an exchange and that he is awaiting acceptance by New France. However, Governor Vaudreuil's envoy Courtemanche fell ill and negotiations are now at a standstill."

"Will our troubles never end?" John groaned.

"We must trust God to help us." Benjamin answered. "In the meantime, let us get you food and drink after your exhausting ordeal. You must be starving and in need of rest."

"That I am and I would appreciate that."

"In the morning we can go to the meeting house and talk to the other people about what you have experienced.

Perhaps we can bring encouragement to some of them if you know the fates of any of their loved ones."

They walked to the temporary shelter where Benjamin and Thankful lived, and after food and drink and more sharing, they retired, John sleeping on a pallet of straw near the fire. He didn't awaken until midday and then went to the Meeting House where others in the village had gathered to hear of his escape and what news he knew of their loved ones.

Chapter Eleven

"Ye are bought with a price: be not the servants of men."

1 Corinthians 7:23

I n the weeks following, Vaudreuil's envoy Courtemanche's health improved and he agreed to return to New France on an English vessel under a flag of truce. The English were delighted with this turn of events which gave them an opportunity to travel French waters and learn how to navigate the difficult waters of the St. Lawrence River that they had previously not known how to sail. Learning these secrets of navigating the difficult parts of the river would give them an advantage over the French.

A Scotsman named Samuel Vetch was the captain of the ship and the brother-in-law of John Livingston who had been the guide for Sheldon and Wells the year earlier. Vetch also spoke French and had business contacts with merchants in New France.

When asked what payment he would demand for his services he replied, "I need no compensation other than that you would grant me permission to bring back French beaver pelts to pay for some debts that I owe." Governor Dudley agreed and sent his own eighteen year old son William as his personal emissary. The plan was that Vetch and Dudley would gather intelligence about the river access to Quebec and observe the city's defenses, should the English decide to launch an invasion.

Vetch and the younger Dudley arrived in Quebec in September of 1705 and began meeting with some of the captives and working to secure their release. Governor Vaudreuil agreed to let them meet with Reverend Williams and his son

Stephen at Chateau Richer several miles up the river from Quebec.

While preparing to leave Quebec, they walked the riverfront by the marketplace to gather provisions for their journey. Vetch was involved with some trade that was not sanctioned by either the French or English governments. His ship was filled with goods that New France desperately needed and he was engaged in negotiating trade with the French merchants for items that the English colonists needed.

While Vetch was involved with his trade negotiations which, though illegal, Governor Vaudreuil apparently was allowing, William Dudley noticed what he thought might be an Englishman. It was hard to tell though because the young man was dressed in Indian garb and had a shaved head with tufts of bristled hair as the Hurons wore. The sandy haired lad was accompanied by his Huron master who stood a few yards away talking to one of the merchants at the market while he was selling vegetables to passers-by.

Dudley approached the boy and whispered, "Are you Indian or one of the English captives?"

"My name is Jonathan Hoyt and I am a captive from Deerfield. My sister Sarah and Ebenezer Nims live with the Hurons at Lorette, a village about eight miles from here and we would all like to go home," he whispered. "Yonder is my adoptive uncle and master Thaovenhosen and perhaps he would let me go if you gave him money," Jonathan suggested. "He is a kind man and treats me well, but I miss my home and family."

"Does he speak French?" Dudley asked.

"Yes, he does as the Catholic priests speak French in our village," Jonathan answered.

Dudley approached Thaovenhosen and spoke to him in his limited French. "Good day, Sir. My name is William Dudley and I am here representing my father Governor Dudley from the Massachusetts Bay colony to arrange for the release of some of our captives. I am prepared to give you twenty dollars in silver if you will grant the release of this young man."

Thinking of his people in the village who were desperate for money to be used for trade with the French, Thaovenhosen impulsively accepted Dudley's offer.

Jonathan immediately left with Dudley and boarded the ship. He had mixed emotions on leaving his master who had never shown anything but kindness to him and was like a father to him. Although he was anxious to return to his home, he regretted not being able to have Sarah and Ebenezer join him. He looked back and saw Thaovenhosen walking slowly away from the market.

Thaovenhosen immediately regretted his hasty decision, as he had grown quite fond of Jonathan and thought of him as a son. He turned around and hurried back to the place where he had made the agreement. He wanted to return the money and retrieve Jonathan, but it was too late. He watched with deep sadness as Jonathan sailed away with the Englishmen, perhaps never to be seen again. He felt an ache in his heart for this boy who had come to mean so much to him.

When Thaovenhosen arrived back at Lorette he walked through the fields and Sarah saw that Jonathan was not with him. Fearing that he had met with some kind of harm while in Quebec, she left her weeding and rushed up to him.

"Where is my brother?" Sarah asked. "Did he come to harm while in Quebec?"

"He is no more." Thaovenhosen grunted as he walked away.

"What do you mean, 'he is no more?'" she pleaded as she ran after him. "Tell me what happened to him!"

"He is no more!" he spat out and kept walking.

Once more Sarah cried out, "Tell me what has happened to my brother Jonathan!"

Thaovenhosen stopped and chokingly uttered, "He left with Boston men."

"He escaped?" she said. "He is not dead?"

"He is no more." Thaovenhosen repeated and entered his longhouse.

Sarah was so excited that she ran to find Ebenezer who was by the river practicing his archery with his master. As soon as he saw her, he asked his master Gassisowangen if he could speak with Sarah. His master nodded his assent, but warned him that he could only talk to her for a moment. Ebenezer left his bow on a stump and joined Sarah who stood several yards away.

"What is it, Sarah? You look excited about something."

"Jonathan has escaped!" she exclaimed. "I don't know the details. Thaovenhosen didn't want to talk about it, but he said that Jonathan left with some men from Boston."

"Do you think that we are going to be rescued as well?" he remarked.

"I don't know, but we must pray that our release will soon follow."

But Dudley and Vetch, after three weeks of negotiations, were only able to secure the release of eleven captives before their return to Boston. Sadly, Sarah and Ebenezer were not among them.

In December of that year Governor Dudley sent a merchant Captain named William Rouse to Arcadia with 47 French prisoners as an act of good faith in hopes that Governor Vaudreuil would release the same number of captives. Because the pirate Baptiste was not among the French prisoners, Rouse was only able to return with seventeen English captives, none of them from Deerfield. He made a second trip and came back with only eight more. Again, sadly, none were from Deerfield.

In January of 1706 almost two years after the raid, Ensign Sheldon, John Wells, Joseph Bradley and two French prisoners travelled by the same route as they had previously taken carrying Governor Dudley's answer to a treaty of neutrality proposed by Vaudreuil. They arrived in New France in March of 1706. The French governor rejected Dudley's response, again dashing the hopes of the Englishmen.

"He has failed to send Baptiste with the French prisoners!" the governor ranted, slamming his fist on his desk. He immediately ordered more attacks on the New England frontier. Negotiations between the two countries stalled and the captives lost hope once more.

The French authorities threatened to put Reverend John Williams into prison and shackle him with iron if Baptiste was not immediately released from prison.

Ensign Sheldon persisted despite these threats and actually made some progress. He was able to meet once more with Reverend Williams who begged him to visit Kahnawake where his daughter Eunice still lived with the nuns at the mission there. The ensign tried to see Eunice, but was refused a meeting with her. He was able to talk to some of the other captives who told him of the persistent efforts by the priests and nuns there to force the captives to be baptized as Catholics and renounce their Puritan beliefs. Most of the younger ones converted, but most of the older ones continued to resist, even though they were subjected to severe punishments for their lack of cooperation.

Finally on May 30, 1706, Sheldon was able to persuade Governor Vaudreuil to release some more of the captives. He set sail for Port Royale, Acadia with forty more English captives. To his delight, one of them was his own son Remembrance and another was his daughter Mary. Again, Ebenezer and Sarah were not among the captives.

In November of that same year Reverend Williams and four of his children were released when the English finally released the pirate Pierre Maisonnat dit Baptiste. But Eunice Williams refused to leave her Indian family at Kahnawake, nearly breaking Reverend Williams' heart.

Chapter Twelve

--- ✤ ---

*"Let us break their bands, and
cast their cords from us."*

Psalms 2:3

After his release, Reverend Williams made several trips back to New France to try and secure the release of his beloved daughter Eunice. He was able to have one short visit with her, but each successive effort was met with failure to even be allowed to see her. On his return from one of his visits to Kahnawake, he went to Quebec to visit Ebenezer and Sarah at Lorette.

"Oh, Reverend Williams, it is so good to see you!" Sarah smiled in greeting when she saw the pastor entering the village. "Do you know if any of my family is safe at home? Did Jonathan make it back safely?" she asked.

"Yes, my child. Jonathan is safe back home and living with your sister Mary who married Judah Wright. Judah was released from captivity last year. You will be happy to learn that your little brother Benjamin also survived the massacre by escaping through a window and hiding in a corn crib. He is safe with the others and has grown tall and strong. At first he was distraught that everyone but him was gone, but then Mary returned from her visit to Hadley after the attackers left our village."

"Oh, my! I just thought he was killed in the raid! I am so happy that he is safe!" she exclaimed. "I am so happy that Judah Wright made it safely back home. He and Mary were planning to marry. I am glad for them. Do you have news of my father and mother?"

"Good news and bad news. Your mother was released with me and arrived in Boston in 1706. She was able to find out that your father did not survive the march after leaving you to go with the Pennacocks. She was able to find solace and comfort when her dear family friend Judge Sewell saw her at the church service we all attended. He was a widower and asked for your mother's hand in marriage and she agreed. She said that she could not face returning to Deerfield where so much tragedy had occurred. They were married quite soon afterwards. I believe that the Lord is blessing that union and bringing both of them comfort. We will continue to pray and take comfort in knowing that we will see all of our loved ones in Heaven if we hold fast to our Christian faith."

"Yes, you are right, Reverend Williams, and I am so happy that my mother has found a small amount of peace after losing so much. I am so sad that my dear father suffered so much after we parted. I have prayed that he made it safely back home. Now we must wait until Heaven before we can be reunited."

Reverend Williams nodded and thought of his own dear wife.

"Have you heard anything about Joseph Alexander?" Sarah asked. "Was he able to escape that first night without harm? I have waited all these years for news from him," she said anxiously. "I fear that he has perished or he would have come for me."

"Oh, my Child, you must understand. Joseph was injured while trying to escape and your friend Margaret Mattoon took care of him. All of her family had perished or been captured and she and Joseph developed a bond while trying to recover from their grief and injuries. Everyone in the village was just doing their best to survive and heal after suffering such terrible losses. People needed to find comfort where they could to get over their grief. Joseph and Margaret married in 1705 and now have a child."

Seeing her look of surprise, he reached out and held her shaking hand, "I am so sorry, my child, but Margaret had no one to care for her and Joseph's home had been destroyed in the raid. Joseph told me to tell you that he is so very sorry that he was unable to fulfill his promise to you and asked for your forgiveness."

Sarah nodded and wiping away a tear said, "If it be the Lord's will, then I will accept it as so."

Ebenezer saw them and asked Gassisowangen if he could leave his work to join the two. His master reluctantly nodded his permission.

"Greetings, Reverend Williams. It is so good to see you! I pray all is well with you and your family. What news do you have of our family and neighbors at home?"

The pastor indicated a log for them to sit on and then told Ebenezer of his family's fate. He shared that his step-brother Zebediah had taken ill while in captivity in Montreal shortly after the earthquake that had struck in March of 1706 and died in April.

"Oh, I'm so sorry to hear about Zebediah! He was such a wonderful brother and loved the Lord," Ebenezer said. "I will miss him dearly."

"Yes, there is quite a story that accompanied his death," Reverend Williams continued. "He would often bring encouragement to the captives near Montreal where he lived on the Island of St. Lawrence, just two miles from where I lived with the Jesuits. He even talked to some of the captives who had been taken in the last war and had fallen into popery and tried to convince them to come back to our faith. This made the priests and other French men enraged, although they all said that he was a good man, one that was very prayerful and who studied the holy scriptures."

"Yes, he taught me much when we lived in Deerfield," Ebenezer reflected.

"He visited me before he went to the hospital in Quebec when he became so ill."

"I wish I could have seen him before he died! If only I had known he was so close!"

"After he died, the French said that Zebediah had been damned and gone to hell. They spread the story that your brother had appeared in flaming fire before an Englishman named Joseph Egerly who was taken in the last war and told him that he was damned for refusing to embrace popery. The priests were angry that after all the pains that had been used to bring him to *the true faith* he had stubbornly refused to convert to their religion. Like your brother, Joseph Egerly had also refused to take up the popish religion and attend mass and partake of communion, so the priests told me that now that Egerly had been visited by Zebediah who had warned him of the dangers of clinging to our false faith, he was now attending mass every day."

"What did you say to this?" Ebenezer asked.

"I told them that I didn't believe the story and that I bless God that our religion didn't need any lies to uphold, maintain and establish it to be true. Then the priests said that God approved of their religion and witnessed miraculously against ours."

"I can't believe that they would spread such an unbelievable story to try and make us choose their religion," Ebenezer observed.

"I told them that I was persuaded that Zebediah's soul was in Heaven and that they were just devising fables to seduce souls. They kept telling me the story was true for several weeks and that they even had witnesses from those who came over the river from the island attesting to the truth of the story. I begged God to refute this hellish design of theirs so that they might not gain even one soul from this abominable lie."

"Did He answer your prayer?"

"After several weeks a man came to the house where I was staying and affirmed that the story was true. He said that Joseph Egerly had been over the river and told one of his neighbors that the story was true. A few hours later, I came across that same neighbor and asked him if he'd seen Egerly lately. He said that he had. Then I asked him what news Egerly had told him and he said 'none'. Then when I told him what they were saying that Egerly had claimed, he laughed and answered that Egerly had said nothing of the sort to him and he was sure that if it had been true, he would have mentioned it."

"That's good," said Ebenezer.

"Yes, and about a week later John Boult, a young lad of about seventeen years who had been captured from Newfoundland, came over from the Island of St. Lawrence to see me. He had often come over with Zebediah to visit me. He was a very serious and sober young lad and was grieving the loss of your brother. He told me that for several weeks the priests had been telling him the same story and that Joseph Egerly was so disturbed by it that he was going to mass every day and that he was so convicted of its truth that he wanted Boult to leave his false religion and come over to popish religion or his damnation would be 'dreadfully aggravated.' He said the priests pressured him day and night so he could get no rest, but he kept telling them that their efforts were contrary to the word of God, that he did not believe what they said, and that he could not embrace their religion. Then he said that one day he was sitting in his house and who should come by, but Egerly."

"Go on."

"Boult said that he asked Egerly in front of his whole family if the story was true."

"What was his answer?" Ebenezer asked eagerly.

"He said that it was a great falsehood and that Zebediah never appeared to him, nor did he ever say such a thing to anyone. He also said that he hadn't been to mass since Zebediah's death. After the lad shared this testimony with me, we prayed to God to deliver us and all the rest of the captives from such delusions and that those who had succumbed to them would be recovered. Then we parted."

"I wish we had known of this at the time," Ebenezer said.

"After the lad left, I took my pen and wrote a letter to Samuel Hill and his brother Ebenezer, the captives from Wells who were in Quebec.

"Yes, I often speak with them," Ebenezer said.

"I had hoped that they would be able to share the letter with you and Sarah, so that you all would be warned of the dangers and be warned of the falsehood of the reports, but the letter fell into the hands of the priests and was never delivered. When I was released, Egerly came home with us, so they gained nothing but shame by their tactics. God often disappoints the crafty devices of deceitful men."

Then Reverend Williams related the story of John's successful escape from Montreal and recent marriage to their step-sister Elizabeth who had been released.

"I am sorry to hear about Zebediah, but am thankful that John made a successful escape and married Elizabeth Hull," Ebenezer said. "She had no one to care for her. And what about Father?" he asked hesitantly, for he feared that the news would not be good.

"Your father also died shortly after the raid," the pastor answered.

"I had hoped that the wound that father received from the French officer while trying to protect our family had been minor and that he had survived," he said with deep sadness, "but I was afraid that it was not so. Perhaps his wounds were more serious than they appeared to me."

"What Benjamin and Thankful said was that they thought he died from a broken heart more than from his wounds. He kept saying that he was being punished for his youthful sins and wouldn't be persuaded that God had forgiven him," Reverend Williams explained.

"Yes, he said that so many times," Ebenezer responded. "He never really forgave himself for his early actions in Northampton and spent the rest of his life trying to make up for them."

"God did forgive him and I'm sure that He is now safe in His presence with all of the others who are now in Heaven with him. Now my children, let us pray that soon you will be allowed to leave and come home."

Sarah then left to bring a simple meal of roast venison and vegetables, and after they ate and then being assured that the two captives were being treated relatively well, Reverend Williams left the two to continue on his journey. "Godspeed, my children," he said in farewell.

They watched him walk away, the only contact they had had from home in all their years of captivity and sat in silence for a few minutes, each in their own thoughts before Ebenezer asked Sarah, "What did you learn of your family? Did Jonathan make it back safely? Is Joseph alright?"

"Jonathan made it back safely and is living with my sister Mary and her husband Judah Wright who was also released.

I also have good news about my little brother Benjamin. He did not perish in the raid as we had all feared."

"Benjamin is alive? I am so relieved to hear this wonderful news! What about Joseph?"

"Joseph is married to Margaret Mattoon," she sighed.

"My sister Thankful's sister-in-law?"

"Yes, it seems that Joseph was wounded when he tried to escape. When he made it back to Deerfield, he found his home in flames and saw Margaret walking around stunned because she was the only one left in her family who hadn't been killed or captured. She took Joseph in and nursed him and they were able to bring each other much comfort. Reverend Stoddard from Northampton married them shortly thereafter because Reverend Williams had been captured, as you know."

"I guess I can understand it all, but I am so sorry, Sarah. I know you were planning on marrying him."

"I guess the Lord has other plans for me," she responded as she rose to return to her work." She had no idea how true those words would be.

Chapter Thirteen

"For they conceive mischief and bring forth vanity, and their belly hath prepared deceit."

Job 15:35

As the months and years wore on, Sarah tended the aging Ashutuaa and tried to make friends with the other young women of the tribe. Most of them treated her with a degree of kindness, but there was one who had taken a fancy to Ebenezer and was jealous of his attention to Sarah. She was Hum-isha-ma, the adopted great granddaughter of Ashutuaa. Hum-isha-ma was the Iroquois captive who had been captured when she was only a child, the one who told the Hurons about how to make maple sugar. She believed that because her adopted great grandmother had such great influence in the tribe and was respected by the members of her village, that she would be able to choose her own mate. Her choice was Ebenezer, although he did not know it.

One late autumn day, Ebenezer was talking with his master's daughters Hatironta and Kondiaronk and teaching them the songs that he used to sing with his own dear sisters. Caught up in their activities, they didn't see Hum-isha-ma striking Sarah and calling her "*kanashwa*", which meant "*slave,*" because Sarah was watching Ebenezer with the young girls instead of tending to extra chores that Hum-isha-ma had given her. Hum-isha-ma felt superior to Sarah because she had been adopted into the tribe, and Sarah was only a slave. Sarah didn't dare react to the cruel attack for fear that Hum-isha-ma would tell Ashutuaa who would make life difficult for her. She went back to her work shucking corn.

Shortly thereafter, Hum-isha-ma did go to Ashutuaa. "That *kanashwa* Sarah is always neglecting her duties and being lazy. We would be better off sending her away from the village at the earliest opportunity, perhaps to be sold to one of the French families in Quebec or Montreal."

Despite the fact that Ashutuaa would be losing her personal slave, she readily agreed to her adopted great-granddaughter's demands.

"Perhaps when we attend the Feast of the Holy Sacrament in the spring we can trade her to one of the French families in Montreal," Hum-isha-ma suggested and her great-grandmother gave her assent. Ashutuaa did not share what she knew in her heart that she would probably not be alive for the Feast of the Holy Sacrament or any other of the Holy Days and would no longer need Sarah's services.

But Hum-isha-ma did not have to wait for months for her plan to take place. Father Meriel, the priest from Montreal and some of the surrounding missions, came to visit Father D' Avaugour.

Hum-isha-ma followed them and stood outside the window of the church where she overheard their conversation.

"There is an officer in Montreal who has requested that I find an English captive to be a companion to his wife, Madame Marguerite de La Rochelle. He is often out on raids against the English and, since his wife's servant has left to join the Sisters of Ursuline at the Convent in Montreal, they have no one there to do the work that is required to maintain their home and help his wife prepare for the social engagements that they are expected to host. He does not want to hire and pay for a French woman or to have an Indian slave or one from the Caribbean because his wife requests that an English captive be procured as her companion," he continued.

"I will consider your request, my friend," Father D' Avaugour replied. "I will have to think about this, but I believe I have just such a person in mind."

"Since he will not be required to pay for her services, he is willing to pay a huge sum to the church here in Lorette should you send a captive woman to care for his wife," Father Meriel said, trying to entice Father D' Avaugour to quickly make a decision.

After hearing this exchange between the two priests, Hum-isha-ma ran to her great-grandmother with the fortuitous news.

"I will talk to Father Meriel immediately, daughter," she said as she started to rise from her fur-covered platform. "Help me to get up and bring me those moccasins that Sarah just finished putting beadwork on to give to Father D' Avaugour. Yes, and some of the apples that she picked this morning. Perhaps he will listen to me."

Hum-isha-ma did as she was bid and followed her great-grandmother to the mission church and stood outside the window listening to her grandmother talk to the priest.

"Father D' Avaugour, please accept this small gift of moccasins and fresh apples from me and listen to my words," she began as she entered the church and gave the sign of the cross and then knelt before the father. My granddaughter Hum-isha-ma happened to be walking just outside the window and overheard your talk with Father Meriel, the priest from Montreal. I am willing to sell my slave Sarah to the French man in Montreal if you will agree to marry my granddaughter Hum-isha-ma to the captive Ebenezer Nims in the spring during the Feast of the Holy Sacrament in Montreal."

"She does not want to marry one of her own, a Huron warrior?" he asked.

"No, she has decided that she wants to wed the captive. It is her right as a Huron woman to choose her mate."

"Yes," agreed the priest. "Sarah is one who does not submit to my efforts to bring her into the one true faith and be baptized. She stubbornly hangs onto her foolish English Puritan beliefs and will not be converted. She said that she made a promise to her father and to Reverend Williams and to God and will not be persuaded to break that vow. Perhaps it would be a good thing for her to be sent to Montreal and away from her friend Ebenezer Nims who also refuses to convert. Maybe we will have better success in their conversion if we separate the two. However, before I will agree to marry your granddaughter to him, we must convince Ebenezer that he must be converted. At the very least, I will insist that any children they have be baptized into the true faith. Does he also desire to marry your granddaughter Hum-isha-ma?"

"I will see that he does," said Ashutuaa as she bid her farewell. "You leave that to me."

Ashutuaa went back to her longhouse and found Hum-isha-ma waiting for the news.

"Father D' Avaugour has agreed to our proposal, Granddaughter," she explained. "However, we must find a way to force Ebenezer to convert to the Catholic faith before the priest will marry you."

"I will think about it," Hum-isha-ma responded as she left her grandmother and went out into the darkening skies of an approaching storm. As she turned the corner at the end of the longhouse she saw Ebenezer laughing and playing with Hatironta and Kondiaronk and an idea began to germinate in her mind of just how she might accomplish her plan.

Chapter Fourteen

"Lord, how are mine adversaries increased? how many rise against me?"

Psalms 3:1

Hum-isha-ma hid in the shadows behind the longhouse and watched as Ebenezer played with the little girls. They were singing the songs that Ebenezer had taught them earlier. She knew that he was still mourning for his sisters that had died in the fire when his village was attacked during the raid.

"He should be doing this with his own children, our children," she thought. "It is only a matter of time before such a thing will happen if my plan is successful."

As the sky grew into a threatening, roiling darkness, Ebenezer told the girls that they must hurry and return to their longhouse before it started to rain. As the thunder and lightning began to fill the angry purple sky Hum-isha-ma approached him.

"I see how much you enjoy playing with Hatironta and Kondiaronk," she said in greeting.

"Yes, I do. They remind me of my own little sisters," he acknowledged.

"Do you ever long for a family of your own?" she asked as she moved closer to him and put her hand on his shoulder.

"I do, but the priest refuses to marry me unless I convert to the Catholic faith."

"Would that be such a terrible thing to do?" she challenged.

"I don't know if I could do such a thing," he responded as he moved away from her touch and rose to get out of the approaching storm.

"Do you have a person in mind that you would choose for your wife?" she pressed, moving closer to him once more.

"Yes, I do, but she also refuses to convert."

"You mean Sarah Hoyt, my grandmother's slave, don't you?" she frowned.

"Yes, I have loved her since we were children, but she was promised to another man from our village, a strong warrior. Now we have heard that he has married another and Sarah may still be mourning that loss. I don't want to press her."

"What if I told you that Sarah just told me that she would be willing to marry you if you would have her?" she said to tantalize him.

"She would be willing to convert to do so?"

"She said that she would if you would."

"I must go to her and see if what you say is true!" he exclaimed. "You will have to talk to her tomorrow," Hum-isha-ma explained. "I just saw her walking to the church to talk to the priests, perhaps to tell them about her decision to convert so that she can marry you," she lied.

He looked and saw Sarah enter the church and had hope that soon she and he could marry. Little did he know that Sarah was indeed inside the church, but not for the reason that Hum-isha-ma shared.

Sarah stood confused and drained of all feelings as she faced the two priests.

"Father Meriel has come to take you to Montreal in the morning," Father D' Avaugour had just told her. "You are to live with a French family there to take care of one of our officer's wives, to be her companion, and also to do household chores for them. Her husband is often at Fort Chambly and other places and does not want her to be left alone. Gather up your belongings and come back to the church where you will sleep tonight so that we can leave at first light without disturbing the others in your longhouse," he continued. "The storm should pass by then."

"Will I be able to say goodbye to Ebenezer, my fellow captive, before I leave?" she asked, choking back sobs? "Surely he will want to know what is to happen to me."

"No, you will not have time as we need to have your help in loading provisions for the journey," Father D' Avaugour answered. "I will tell him at Mass in the morning. Go quickly now as Father Meriel wishes to get an early start and wants to retire early."

Sarah was stunned at the news and regretted that she would not be able to say goodbye to Ebenezer. She quickly ran through the pounding rain and howling wind back to the longhouse and told Ashutuaa of the priests' plan. Thinking that Ashutuaa would be disappointed that she would be leaving and no longer there to serve her, she couldn't understand why the old woman had the hint of a smile on her withered face. She gathered up her Bible and other few belongings and wrapped them in a covering of deerskin to keep them dry in the storm. She searched for Ebenezer, but Hum-isha-ma had led him away from her sight telling him they must hurry and take shelter before the fast approaching storm.

Ebenezer spent the night in the longhouse listening to the rain pounding heavily on the roof. In the distance he heard thunder and saw flashes of lightning through the hole in the ceiling where the smoke from the constantly burning fire was trying to escape. He prayed for wisdom, asking God to show him what he should do about conversion to the Catholic faith in order to marry his beloved Sarah.

After a sleepless night, he finally fell asleep just as the pale light of dawn crept into the village. He was surprised when he awoke to find that he was the only one left in the longhouse.

Knowing that his master would be scolding him if he didn't show up for his daily chores, he skipped his morning meal and ran into Gassisowangen who was just entering the longhouse to find him after attending morning Mass.

"Hurry. We must go to the river and catch fish today. You are late. You missed Mass this morning. Father D' Avaugour said that he wants to talk to you when we get back this afternoon. We must go while the lingering clouds from last night's storm shade the water so the fish cannot see us and hide themselves. Grab your spear and come now."

Ebenezer had hoped to talk to Sarah, but spent the day fishing instead. When he and Gassisowangen returned bringing back several fish, he saw Father D' Avaugour walking towards him. He thought that the priest was going to chastise him for missing Mass and he knew that he would be expected to confess his sin, but he was also hopeful that the priest would be bringing the good news that he and Sarah could marry.

"My master Gassisowangen said that you would like to talk to me. I am ready to confess my sin for missing Mass. I did not sleep well during the storm and overslept. Would you join me as I bring some fish to Sarah to clean for Ashutuaa?" he asked. "I am sure she would like to have fresh fish for her meal tonight. I have some for you as well Father," he added, hoping to deflect the censure of the priest and move on to the subject that was closest to his heart.

"Ebenezer, Sarah is gone," Father D' Avaugour replied.

"Gone? What do you mean? Where has she gone? Is she with the other women gathering herbs or in the fields perhaps?" he asked.

"No. She left this morning with Father Meriel. She will not come back. She will live in Montreal with a French family from now on."

"What is this you are saying? But she didn't even say good-bye!" he objected. "Why didn't she come and see me before she left?"

"Father Meriel wanted to get an early start so they could make it to Trois-Rivières before dark in case another storm approached. He had to tend to some matters there before continuing on. They must hurry because she must be in Montreal to care for the young wife of one of the officers in Montreal. Her husband needs to go to Fort Chambly and has no one to stay with his wife. He may already have had to leave her alone and wants someone there immediately."

"But, I was going to ask her to marry me!" Ebenezer lamented. "I thought that she was going to tell you that she was willing to convert to your faith so that we could marry and have children of our own. I was going to tell you that I was prepared to finally convert to Catholicism so that you would agree to marry us, but now I see that God has given me His answer that He doesn't want me to give up my Puritan faith, even to marry the woman I love."

Hum-isha-ma overheard them talking and realized that she would have much more work to do before her plans would come to fruition.

Chapter Fifteen

"For I know the thoughts, that I have thought towards you, saith the Lord, even the thoughts of peace, and not of trouble, to give you an end, and your hope."

Jeremiah 29:11

Sarah stepped into the canoe in the early morning light carrying only her few belongings in a bundle made of deerskin. She grieved that she would be leaving her dear friend Ebenezer, her only contact with the life she had known so long ago. As they travelled on the wide river, she recalled the first time they had come this way. It seemed like a lifetime ago, a time when she had hoped that they would soon be sent home or that her beloved Joseph would come and rescue her. Those futile hopes were soon dashed and the reality of her life set in. She had grown accustomed to the daily routine of life in an Indian village, and although very foreign to her, it soon became familiar. It would never be her home, but she would always cling to her memories of her dear family and friends, wherever they may now be.

She sat low in the canoe and listened to the rhythm of the oars as the Indians paddled through the swiftly flowing waters. Occasionally she heard the cries of mourning doves in the trees along the shore. "*I, too, am mourning, little doves,*" she thought as she wiped tears from her eyes.

Soon she was asleep, for she had not slept well because of the storm the night before. She was awakened by the slowing of the boat and the voices of the men as they arrived in Trois-Rivières. She disembarked with the others and walked stiffly up the bank. She hoped that she would see some of the captives from Deerfield, but was not able to see any of them. After waiting while Father Meriel met with the Ursuline nuns at the convent there, they had a light meal then were shown to their rooms at the mission where they would spend the night. In the early morning, she was awakened by one of the sisters and after a simple breakfast of fruit and bread and cheese, they continued on their journey to Montreal.

She had missed seeing Ebenezer's young sister Abigail and the boy Josiah Rising who were then living in Trois-Rivières with the Ursuline nuns and had been baptized by Father Meriel with the names Ignace Raizenne and Marie Elisabeth Nims shortly after their capture in 1704. She hadn't realized that the reason the priest had met with the nuns without her was that he wanted them to keep the children out of her sight. He didn't want her to write to Ebenezer and let him know where his sister was because he feared that Ebenezer would try and escape to find her and take her home.

Several days later they arrived in Montreal, and passing through the busy wharf at the market place with all the bustling activity from the merchants, traders, nuns and missionaries, sailors, soldiers, and Indians from all tribes, Sarah noticed the French ladies in their beautiful silk gowns with beads and embroidered accents and fancy gold or silver jewelry adorning their fingers and necks. Under their gowns were layers of petticoats and what looked like cages under their skirts which gave their hips an extended roundness that was very foreign to Sarah. She had only worn simple English gowns or Indian dresses made of deerskin that hung naturally from her slim waist. Several of the ladies wore elaborate hairdos or fancy lace caps. She felt out of place in her simple deerskin dress and wondered if she would be given other clothes or would be allowed to sew something herself out of linen or wool perhaps.

Seeing a horse and carriage up the street from the wharf, Father Meriel bid Sarah to follow him as he hailed the driver. He made arrangements for the man to take them the few miles to the de la Rochelle home where Sarah was to stay. The priest pointed out a school which was founded by the Sisters of the Congregation de Notre-Dame in 1670 for the education of the Indian and French girls in the city. He also showed her the hospital that the Ursuline Sisters had established for the care of the sick and the massive Notre-Dame Church, the most imposing building in the city.

"On the way here you told me that Madame de La Rochelle was ailing, Father Meriel. Does she need to go to the hospital or will I care for her in her home?"

"Her only sickness appears to be a heart that longs to be with her husband and to have a child. She grieves that she has not been able to bring a child to full term. She has not been able to adjust well to the rigors of life in New France with her husband often being away for months at a time. That is why she wanted an English girl because she knows that you are all taught to read at an early age so that you can read the Bible. She had learned of the English captives living in the Quebec area and thought one would be suitable. That is why the priest in Lorette and I decided to send you to her."

"How old is Madame de La Rochelle?" Sarah asked.

"She is in her early thirties. I think you will enjoy living with her. She will need your help in conducting some of her social engagements that are expected of a French officer's wife. You will be required to do sewing and repairing of her clothing--and most likely some for yourself at first so you fit into society here in Montreal!" he exclaimed, viewing her rugged native dress. She orders some of her fancier garments from Europe or sometimes from tailors in Quebec or Montreal, but they will require fitting and finishing which you will be expected to do."

Sarah wondered if she would have to fashion whatever the contraption was that the women at the river wore beneath their skirts. If so, she would have to learn how to do so.

Father Meriel continued, "I don't approve of the women's wearing of immodest and expensive clothing in styles beyond their status and some of them even wear short skirts at mid-calf length with jackets rather than gowns, but you will be happy to know that Madame de La Rochelle dresses relatively modestly and usually wears just a cap to cover her hair rather than having her hair elaborately coiffed. That is, unless she is attending a fancy social engagement where she would be expected to wear the latest European hair do," he added.

Sarah was relieved to learn that she wouldn't be required to make the fancy silk dresses that she had seen at the marketplace when she first arrived. She felt comfortable in being able to do the finishing work on any of Madame de La Rochelle's clothing as she had learned to do needlework at an early age. All the young girls in her village were taught to do sewing and needlework by their mothers. They started by learning to embroider simple things like pillowcases and handkerchiefs, then learned to do more intricate work. Sarah learned how to spin wool into yarn, how to mend clothing, and make quilts and other household items from her mother.

She thought about some of the other duties that she would probably need to do for Madame de La Rochelle. They would probably include weaving cloth, spinning wool and flax into yarn for making hats, mittens and stockings for the cold winters in New France. Of course she would also do embroidery, quilting, and mending, all tasks in which she was skilled. After spending the last several years laboring in the fields and cooking over a smoky fire in the longhouse, she was actually looking forward to her new duties. She hoped that Madame de La Rochelle would be easier to please than Ashutuaa and her adopted great granddaughter Hum-isha-ma were.

As it was beginning to get dark, they arrived at the home of Lieutenant and Madame de La Rochelle, a lovely stone house surrounded by large trees now turning red and gold. It was unusual to see a stone house as most of those she had seen on her way were built of wood from the surrounding forests. In the dim light she saw beautiful flower gardens that were just finishing their season. Sarah was both nervous and excited to begin her new life with this new family.

As Father Meriel helped her out of the carriage she spotted a young lady dressed in a quilted vest, a long skirt and a simple petticoat. Her dark brown hair was covered with a simple cap adorned with lace. Around her shoulders she wore a colorful neckerchief which she had tucked into the front of her simple gown. Her feet were covered in simple cloth slippers. With brown eyes sparkling, she smiled at Sarah in welcome.

"Oh, you must be the woman that Father Meriel has fetched to stay with me and help me while my husband is away!" she exclaimed as she grabbed Sarah's hand. "I am so happy that you have arrived safely! My name is Madame de La Rochelle, but please call me 'Marguerite'. What is your name?"

"Sarah, Sarah Hoyt," she answered.

"Please come in and we can talk while you rest from your journey. We have so much to talk about!" Madame de la Rochelle exclaimed.

With that, Father Meriel bid them goodbye and said that he would see them at Mass on Sunday.

Sarah followed Madame de La Rochelle into their warm, spacious house which was furnished in beautiful tapestries and hand carved furniture from Europe. Alongside one wall was a massive fireplace used for heating. Madame de La Rochelle motioned for Sarah to sit in one of the sea green brocade chairs in front of the fireplace and she sat in the one opposite, curling her legs under her.

"My husband had to leave for Fort Chambly yesterday," she explained. "You have arrived just in time to keep me company. Do you know how to cook? she asked. "Oh, but of course you do! All English women in the colonies know how to prepare meals. I have never learned to cook. When I was a young girl I lived at Fort Chambly with my parents. My mother always had a cook to prepare our meals.

When I was a child there I met my husband, Charles. Both of our mothers had come from France to marry soldiers and were friends. After our parents died, Charles and I married and moved to this home so that we could have a home in the city. We wanted to raise our children away from the fort once the wars began again. We had a young French girl who used to live with us but she left to enter the convent of the Congregation de Notre-Dame. She served us well for five years and then desired to become a part of the work with the Sisters of Ursuline. She was a wonderful cook and always prepared dishes that pleased my husband, but I would love to have some simple cooking tonight!"

"Yes, I can cook for you, Madame,"

"Marguerite," she corrected.

"Marguerite."

"Before he left for Fort Chambly my husband left us some salmon and some corn that he bought from the Indians at the market. He said that you should prepare it for our meal when you arrive. I have been eating some bread and leftover venison, but am hungry for salmon. What do you say we get started on something to eat, as I imagine that you must be quite hungry after your long journey."

Sarah agreed and stooped in front of the fireplace and scooped out some of the coals onto the brick hearth to begin her preparations for their dinner.

"Oh, no, Sarah," Madame de La Rochelle said as she linked arms with Sarah and led her into the kitchen. "We have another fireplace here that we use exclusively for meal preparation. This way if we have guests, they do not need to see the mess in the kitchen!" Sarah could not believe such an extravagance, but was happy to know that she could have a place to work away from any of the de La Rochelle's guests when they were entertaining.

Her mistress showed her where the salmon and vegetables and other items were and Sarah began preparing the meal. She placed the salmon and corn in cast iron pots and raked the coals around the pots to begin cooking while she cut up a loaf of bread. She noticed that there were no more loaves in the pantry and so she would need to make more bread or biscuits in the morning.

Also, unless she could find some stored somewhere in the larder, she would have to go to the market for more vegetables at her earliest opportunity. She also noticed that there was no butter for the bread and so she would have to see about churning more for the next meals. She would look outside in the morning to see if they had any livestock. She especially hoped that they would have a cow for milk and butter and also chickens for eggs, but that would have to wait as Madame de La Rochelle kept interrupting her thoughts with her animated chatter. She wondered if because her mistress was alone most of the time, that she had a need to have someone around just to listen to her talk!

Sarah was often accused of being overly talkative herself and was delighted to have someone who could carry on a conversation. She had no one other than Ebenezer to talk to all the time she was in Lorette and he was often not around.

When he was in the Huron village, he spent a lot of his time with his master's little girls Hatironta and Kondiaronk because they were often neglected and left on their own. Hum-isha-ma was supposed to care for them as their mother had died when they were just babies, but she usually found other activities to amuse herself, feeling that it was beneath her to have to care for other people's children.

When the food was done cooking, Sarah placed it on a china plate that she recognized as the same pattern as one that her mother had, that now lay in pieces back at home. It must have come from England rather than France. It made Sarah a little less homesick to be able to see something so familiar. When she had finished setting the food out for Marguerite de La Rochelle she reached for a pewter plate for her own meal to eat away from her mistress.

"What are you doing, Sarah?" Madame de la Rochelle asked. "Please set a place for yourself across from me. We will dine together so we can continue with our visit." Because she was considered a slave, Sarah had always had to eat whatever food was left after everyone else had eaten when she lived with the Hurons back in Lorette.

"Do you play an instrument?" Madame de La Rochelle asked as they got up from the table. "I play the harpsichord and we have a guitar or violin that my husband will play at times. He often desires that we entertain his fellow soldiers and their wives at our home and some of them bring their flutes and guitars and we enjoy an evening of music and dancing. Of course, you will be a part of these festivities when Charles returns from Fort Chambly at Christmas, but tonight I would love to have you join me in playing some tunes. Perhaps you know some English ones that you could teach me?

"Unfortunately I do not play an instrument, but I do love to sing," Sarah replied as she cleaned the table and washed off the dishes. She remembered the way she and Ebenezer used to sing the Psalms they had learned in the village school when they were young children. "Perhaps you can play while I sing." Soon the two young ladies were singing some of the songs that each had learned from the other and the night passed pleasantly."

After an enjoyable evening, Sarah was shown to her room up the stairs. It was furnished with a four poster feather bed covered with a colorful quilt. On the feather pillow was a linen chemise that Marguerite had set out for her to use as a nightshift. Next to it was a cap to keep her head warm in the cool room. A bedside table contained a candlestick with a fresh new candle and a Geneva Bible like the one she carried with her. Across the room was a chest for her things, a small writing desk, another table with a wash basin and pitcher filled with water and a chamber pot on the floor beside the table. Sarah couldn't believe such luxury after having spent years sleeping on the hard platforms covered with animal skins along the edge of the smoky longhouse. She was afraid that she would wake up in the morning and find that it was all a dream. She hadn't had such luxuries since her family had left their house to move into their temporary shelter inside the stockade in Deerfield. Even though Sarah didn't like change, perhaps life in Montreal would not be so bad.

But then she thought of Deerfield. Would she ever see her home again? She drifted off to sleep dreaming of a time when everything seemed as if life would go on as it always was, never changing.

Chapter Sixteen

"She seeketh wool and flax, and laboreth cheerfully with her hands.

She is like the ships of merchants: she bringeth her food from afar."

Proverbs 31:13-14

Awakening to the sounds of birds singing in the huge maple trees that were now turning bright gold and red, Sarah at first couldn't remember where she was. She hadn't slept so comfortably since being dragged from her bed that fateful night so many years ago. She suddenly realized with a flutter in her heart that she was now starting a new life in a place even more distant from her home in Deerfield and must begin her new duties immediately.

She quickly slipped out of the linen chemise that Madame de La Rochelle had so thoughtfully left on her bed the day before and pulled her deerskin garment over her head. She splashed cool water over her face and hands after using the chamber pot that was so conveniently located near the dressing table. How pleasant it was to have the luxury of taking care of her personal needs in the privacy of her own room rather than having to do it outdoors in public as she had grown accustomed to doing while living with the Hurons in Lorette!

Humming one of the Psalms she and Madame de La Rochelle had sung the night before, Sarah found a brush on the dressing table and for the first time in years, had the luxury of fully brushing out her long hair. Instead of braiding it into two long braids as she had done at Lorette, she twisted it into a knot and covered it with a cap similar to the one her mistress wore the day before. She assumed that Madame de La Rochelle had graciously left it on the dressing table for her use.

Peering through the window tucked beneath the sloping roof, she was pleased to see that the back of the house was enclosed by a wooden fence and had a small herb garden like those found in her village in Deerfield. In the back of the property was a chicken coop and a small barn. She heard the moos of cows coming from the barn and was delighted to know that she would have milk and cream for churning butter as well as meat and eggs close at hand. Perhaps she could trade some of the eggs and milk for fresh vegetables or plant a garden in the spring. Then they could have pumpkin, corn and squash. She had learned how to grind corn while with the Hurons to eat during the winter months. She would talk to her mistress about that this morning over breakfast.

She tiptoed quietly down the stairs so as not to wake Madam de La Rochelle and let herself out the back door to gather eggs and cream for breakfast. She was delighted to discover that grazing down a hill behind the barn were a few sheep. She would have wool for spinning into yarn for making warm clothing for the coming winter!

When she came back into the house she built up the fire in the fireplace and placed the freshly gathered eggs into a pot of water and placed it over the coals. Then she went to the larder which was in a lean-to at the back of the house where she found flour which Madame de La Rochelle must have purchased from the market. The Indians had recently begun selling wheat to the residents of Montreal and the French had then milled the grain into flour for the women of Montreal to use in their baking.

She looked further and found the crock holding the dough starter and measured some out to make some fresh bread. After kneading the dough and placing it under a cloth to rise, she cut the remaining loaf of bread left from the last baking and set out freshly churned butter and jam. As soon as the table was set and the food placed on the plates, Madame de La Rochelle came down the stairs to join her for breakfast.

"Oh, how lovely! You have prepared breakfast for us! I would have helped you, but I didn't hear that you had arisen. I was in my room reading my Bible. Did you see the Bible left for you, Sarah?"

"Yes, thank you for that and for the other items that you so thoughtfully provided for me. I have the Bible that my father gave me as we were being separated on the march to New France. His grandfather brought it from England when he came to the colonies in the last century. When my father gave it to me, it was the last time I saw him and I did not know his whereabouts until my pastor Reverend Williams told me that he had died of starvation with the Pennacocks. Reverend Williams' son Steven had also left with them, but he was with a different group of Pennacocks and didn't continue on with my father and his captors. When my father left us, my brother Jonathan, my dear friend Ebenezer and I were led away with our Huron masters to Lorette. My mother was taken to Montreal but she was released a few years ago and married a dear friend she had known in Boston. I had hoped to have seen her again, but the last I saw her she was walking into the forest with her captors and disappeared into the foggy mist, like a disappearing ghost."

"Oh, my! It has been so difficult for you. Were there any others of your family that didn't survive this horrible ordeal?"

"My baby sister and younger brother were killed on the march because they couldn't keep up and my other brother Jonathan was rescued by Governor Dudley's son and a man from our village. His master, Thaovenhosen, sold him for twenty dollars in silver and then immediately regretted his hasty consent. He tried to go back and get Jonathan and return the money but the ship was sailing away out of sight and it was too late. He loved my brother like his own son. He saved his life when the other Indians wanted to kill him to avenge the death of their Great Chief who was killed when they attacked our village. I recently received news that others in my family survived the raid and are living at home in Deerfield."

"Oh, my dear Sarah! I did not know how much you have suffered. I am so sorry. Perhaps someday I can help you to find your way back home. In the meantime, let us ask the Lord to bless this meal and then, after we eat, we must see to finding you some decent clothes to wear."

They ate their breakfast and Sarah sat silently listening to Madam de La Rochelle go on and on about fabrics and the latest dress styles from Europe.

"We must make you a gown to wear for when my husband Charles returns from Fort Chambly," she said. "Do you know how to sew, Sarah?"

When Sarah acknowledged that, yes, she was quite proficient with the needle and thread and also knew how to spin and weave, her mistress was delighted.

"First we must see to it that you have proper dress for attending Mass and then we will see to making you a finer gown. I have some silk from Europe in a pretty blue color that would look lovely with your stunning blue-green eyes and golden red hair!" she exclaimed. "In the meantime, you must wear some of my dresses. I believe that we are close to the same size, although you may be a bit smaller than I am. Perhaps you could take in the seams to make them fit? I will give you some shoes to replace the moccasins that you are wearing so that you will be in fashion here in the city."

Sarah was overwhelmed with the kindness being shown to her by Madame de La Rochelle and quietly nodded her assent. Changing the subject she asked, "Do you think it would be possible for me to go to the market and purchase some vegetables for our meals today?"

"Oh, that would be a wonderful idea!"

"Perhaps I could gather some eggs and trade them with the Indians for squash and corn and beans," Sarah suggested.

"Oh, no, Sarah! That will not be necessary. My husband left some silver that we can use to buy whatever we need. We can also purchase some more fabric from the merchants down at the wharf. This should be a fun adventure for us. I usually don't accompany my husband when he trades at the market. Let us clean up these dishes from the wonderful breakfast you prepared and you can help me hitch up the horses to our carriage and then we can be on our way!"

After finding a suitable dress for Sarah from amongst her many clothes, Madame de La Rochelle looked at her with admiration. "This will do fine!" she exclaimed. "Let us now go to the barn and hitch up Horace and Babette to our carriage and begin our adventure!"

"Do you think we will be safe without escorts down at the market?" Sarah worried. "When Father Meriel and I passed through there on the way to your home, it looked frighteningly busy. Perhaps we should delay our shopping until we can find a man to accompany us there," she suggested, but Madame de la Rochelle wouldn't be persuaded to wait once the idea occurred to her.

So the two young women hitched up the horses and proceeded to travel the dirt road down to the bustling market. Sarah prayed a quick prayer for safety as she took the reins. Her mistress chattered the whole three miles into town and Sarah let her mind drift to thoughts of Ebenezer and home.

Chapter Seventeen

"And I desire you somewhat the more earnestly, that ye so do, that I may be restored to you more quickly."

Hebrews 13:19

E benezer left the village and walked down to the river by the falls. He had thought that by now Sarah would be his bride, but now he was alone, the only English person left in the village. He was consumed with thoughts of his dear Sarah and went quietly about his tasks. Hum-isha-ma continued to pursue him and told him that he must forget about Sarah, the "*kanashwa*", the slave. She told him that now he was Huron and must take a Huron wife. Ebenezer resisted her attempts to entice him and left her and went to practice his archery.

He wanted so much to talk to Sarah, to find out if she had made it safely to her new home in Montreal, but he had only birch bark and a charred stick with which he could write a letter. He saw the priest Father D' Avaugour as he passed by the mission church and asked him for permission to write to her.

"Come inside, my son. Let us talk. Have you re-considered converting to the one true faith?"

"I have considered, Father, but the Lord has not told me to abandon my Puritan faith and until He does, I must remain as I am."

"But you are now a member of the Hurons here in Lorette and have been adopted into the family. All of the Hurons are members of the Catholic faith and are happy to worship God in this way. Why do you continue to resist? We worship the same God, read the same Bible. What is it about our religion that you so detest?' he argued.

"Yes, it is true that we worship the same God, but it is your form of worship that is foreign to me. We Puritans have a simpler way to honor God and do not need all the ceremonies and adornments that your church uses. We also do not celebrate Mass in the way that you do. We do not believe that the bread and wine are the actual body and blood of Christ, but are just symbols used in our Communion service. There are many other practices that we do not share and so I must remain true to the faith of my father and grandfather who came to the New World for religious freedom."

"Perhaps someday you will see that we are not so different," the priest admitted. "Now, what is it that you desire for me to do for you, my son?"

"If it would be possible, I would like to have some parchment and a quill and ink so that I might write to Sarah in Montreal and inquire as to her well-being there," he answered. "Perhaps we might send it with one of the traders that travel the river?"

"I think that can be allowed," the priest said as he reached into his desk for the writing materials. "You can take the letter to the market in Quebec the next time you and Gassisowangen go there to sell vegetables, but let us continue our dialogue about our faith," he said in dismissal.

Ebenezer thanked the priest and went to the river. As he listened to the pounding of the water falling behind him, he found a flat rock and sat down to pen his letter to Sarah.

Lorette, New France
October 2, 1709

"Dearest Sarah,

I pray that this letter finds you safe and well in your new home so far away in Montreal. I must say that I was shocked and in much distress when I discovered that you had left so suddenly without even a chance to say goodbye. You were my only tie to home and I miss you ever so much. I had something I wanted to discuss with you before you left and was on my way to find you when Hum-isha-ma told me that you had been summoned to the mission church to talk to Father D' Avaugour and Father Meriel. I guess it was not the Lord's will for me to be able to see you and I must accept this as His perfect will for me, for us, dear Sarah.

Everything here is as it was when you were with me. Most of the other captives in the area have either been released or have decided to stay and become permanent residents of New France as either French citizens or as members of their Indian families. I still hold fast to our hope that someday we can return to our home and see our family and neighbors there. I know that you share this hope and dream with me, Sarah.

It has been six years since the time when the Indians captured my brothers. In February it will be six years since our lives were so tragically and drastically changed. I hope it is not to be like this forever, but if it is the Lord's desire, then we must learn to be content in whatever state in which we find ourselves, just as the apostle Paul wrote in Philippians.

I have learned that my young sister Abigail remains at Trois-Rivières with Josiah Rising. They have both converted to the Catholic faith. They were too young when we were captured and were easily persuaded to abandon the faith of our people. Eunice Williams is still at Kahnawake near you and so are a few other captives, I know not which ones. I think Mercy Carter may be there as well. Speaking of converting to Catholicism, the father here continues to press me, but there is only one reason why I would do so, but it matters not anymore.

Please write to me if you have an opportunity. If you receive this letter, then it means that I was able to convince one of the traders to deliver it to you.

I pray for you every day, dear Sarah. I hope you do the same for me. May God hold you in the palm of His hand and bless you abundantly.

Your friend and fellow captive who holds your heart captive in my hand,

Ebenezer

Sarah and Madame de La Rochelle pulled into the market area on the wharf where they encountered the same bustling activity that Sarah had experienced on her arrival in Montreal. Leaving their carriage and horses with a young Indian boy who promised to feed and water the horses and stay with them while the women examined the various wares displayed by the merchant, they made their way to a stand where a myriad of dresses, fabrics and notions were on display. Madame de La Rochelle was immediately captivated by an emerald green quilted fabric.

"Look, Sarah. What do you think of this beautiful fabric? It would make a nice waistcoat and skirt for you to wear to Mass, don't you agree? It would complement your beautiful eyes and stunning hair. Let us purchase this and some shoes for you as well," she offered. "I have several caps that you can wear, but let us also buy one of these for tomorrow, don't you think?"

Sarah was overwhelmed with her new mistress's generosity and could never think of repaying her. She would have to do extra chores and pay her back with a listening ear and companionship, which Madame de La Rochelle seemed to crave.

"Perhaps we should attend to the purchase of our vegetables now, Madame," she answered after agreeing to accept the kind offer.

"'*Marguerite*,'" she corrected, then, "No, we must purchase some undergarments for you and then some finer fabric for your gown, perhaps some silk? Yes, I think silk would be exquisite!"

Sarah was not too sure she wanted to buy such finery as she had never worn such costly items of clothing. Silk was forbidden in her former life. The Puritans thought that it was a sin to wear such pretentious clothing. She wondered what her pastor Reverend Williams would think of her if he saw her dressed so extravagantly. "*And Ebenezer! What would he think?*" she mused.

Just as she was thinking of her pastor, she thought she saw him coming up from the river and being greeted by Father

Meriel. She made an apology to Madame de La Rochelle and explained that she must go and greet the dear man.

Her mistress smiled, "But of course, Sarah. I would also like to meet him and thank Father Meriel for bringing me such a wonderful companion." She took Sarah by the arm and the two approached the men.

"Sarah!" Reverend Williams exclaimed. "I am so surprised to see you in Montreal. I had not heard that you were here. Are you and Ebenezer visiting?"

"No, Pastor," she answered. "Let me introduce you to my new mistress, Madame de La Rochelle."

"The wife of Lieutenant Charles de La Rochelle? he asked.

"Yes, the very one," she replied.

"Well, I am very pleased to make your acquaintance, Madame de La Rochelle. I have met your husband and he appears to be a man of honor."

"Thank you, Reverend Williams. Sarah has told me about you and your distress over not being able to bring your daughter, Eunice, I believe that is her name, home.

"Yes, it now seems that I must release her to God and know that He will keep her safe. Despite all my efforts and prayers, it is time that I submit to God's will for her," he said quietly as he turned away to hide his grief.

'You must come and dine with us tonight," Madame de La Rochelle invited. "Sarah and I are just finishing up our purchases here at the market. Would you enjoy some fish or pork, or perhaps a bit of chicken? We are purchasing vegetables and would love to have you join us for supper. We welcome you too, Father Meriel. I want to extend my deepest gratitude to you for bringing me such a delightful companion in Sarah."

Reverend Williams looked to Father Meriel who said, "We would be delighted to join you ladies for supper tonight. Chicken sounds good to me, Reverend Williams. What do you think?"

Williams agreed and Father Meriel asked, "is six o'clock too early for us to arrive?"

"That will be splendid," Madame de La Rochelle answered. "Sarah and I will hurry back and begin our preparations. We look forward to an evening of conversation with you both, don't we Sarah?"

Sarah was eager to hear of any news from home and looked forward to the evening with her beloved pastor.

The women quickly made their purchases and headed back to their carriage where Madame de La Rochelle thanked the young man who had cared for her horses and gave him a few coins to spend at the market.

Chapter Eighteen

—— ✑ ——

"I thank my God, having
you in perfect memory"

Philippians 1:3

The women arrived home and began preparations for the coming meal. Sarah went out to the chicken coop and captured a hen and began plucking it while still outside. She brought it in and cut it up, added some beans, squash, and onions to make a fine soup and placed it in a brass pot which she hung on a notched metal rod which was attached to a horizontal brace in the fireplace so she could move the pot closer to or away from the fire. While the soup was cooking, she placed the risen bread dough into baking pans to place in the brick oven that she had discovered just outside the back door.

While Sarah attended to these tasks, Madame de La Rochelle looked through her chest for a dress for Sarah to wear during their supper.

A few hours later, with the table set and the smell of the supper wafting through the house, the two ladies heard talking as Father Meriel and Reverend Williams alighted from their carriage. The women welcomed them and after polite greetings, the four sat down to eat their meal. Reverend Williams asked if he could ask the Lord to bless their food and their time together, and Father Meriel nodded his assent.

After a pleasant meal where she caught up on news from home from Reverend Williams, Sarah put away leftovers to send with the men and joined the others who had retired to the chairs by the fire.

"Will you be visiting Ebenezer at Lorette before you return to Deerfield?" Sarah asked her pastor as she took a seat on a stool near the fireplace where she could tend the fire.

"I had planned on doing so and thought that I would see you both," he commented.

"Do you think it would be possible for me to send a letter to him before you leave?" she asked.

"Of course, my dear girl," he responded. "I will stop by in the morning on my way home to retrieve it from you."

Father Meriel stood and thanked the women for their hospitality and Reverend Williams did the same. They bid the ladies farewell and went to stay with the Jesuit priests where Reverend Williams often stayed on his visits to Montreal.

After the men left, Sarah went to the kitchen area to finish cleaning up after the meal. When she was done, she asked Madame de La Rochelle if she would mind if she retired early so that she could write a letter to her fellow captive in Lorette.

"But, of course, my dear! Is he a special friend, perhaps?"

"Yes, he is," Sarah replied. "He and I have known each other since we were children. He has always been a kind and faithful companion and a great source of strength for me as we have endured the many hardships of captivity."

"I am sorry that you have been taken away from him," Madame de La Rochelle responded, "but perhaps you can meet someone here in your new home that will take his place in your heart?" she suggested.

"Oh, I'm not sure that will happen," Sarah objected.

"My husband knows many soldiers who would be delighted to have such a beauty as you are on his arm! Maybe he will bring one with him when he comes home for the Christmas holidays. He often brings officers who are not married home with him to ease their loneliness. In the meantime, please go to your room and write to your friend Ebenezer. I will do the same and pen a letter to Charles as it has been awhile since I have done so. You will find writing materials on the writing desk in your room. Goodnight, Sarah. Tomorrow we can begin making your new garments for you to wear to Mass."

Sarah thanked her for her kindness as she climbed the stairs behind her mistress. Of course, she wasn't interested in meeting any French officers, but she was amused at Madame de La Rochelle's efforts to make her comfortable in her new surroundings.

Finding the writing materials in the desk, she penned the following letter:

> *Montreal, New France*
> *October 28, 1709*
>
> *"Dear Ebenezer,*
>
> *I hope that this letter finds you well. I know you must have been shocked to find me gone the day I left. I wanted to find you and let you know that I would be leaving, but I had to hurry in the storm to the mission church where the priests were waiting for me.*

I searched for you in the darkness, but you were nowhere to be found, just like Solomon's bride. Perhaps it is better this way for if I had seen you, I might not have been able to leave.

You must know that I have safely arrived in Montreal. I have not met Lieutenant Charles de La Rochelle, *but his wife Marguerite is very kind to me. I am thankful that I have learned to speak French while living with the Hurons, so that I can understand most of what Madame de la Rochelle says. She talks a lot and very quickly, so I only catch part of what she says.*

I asked her how long she had been in New France and she told me that she was born at Fort Chambly. You remember that we stopped there on our journey here and the kind French woman fed us and let us sleep in her warm home. She told me that her mother was one of the nearly 800 "filles du roi" *or* "King's Daughters" *sent here in the1660's and 70's by King Louis XIV to marry French colonists and soldiers to populate the French colony. The soldiers had been becoming restless and wanted to leave New France and return home where they could marry and settle down. The king wanted them to remain in New France so that he could have a force there to fight the English and the Iroquois and protect France's interest in the New World. The "filles du roi" were held to very high moral standards and had to have a letter from their parish priest attesting to their impeccable character. The king paid for their passage, gave them a trousseau, and a dowry so that the women would be encouraged to marry.*

Madame de la Rochelle's mother's parents were nobles in France who had recently died. She was not their heiress as she had several older brothers, and the oldest would inherit the property and estate. When King Louis sent out the invitation for women of good repute to move to New France, her mother answered the call. Because she was of high birth in France, rather than marrying a farmer as many of the other King's Daughters were, she was matched with an officer, Madame de la Rochelle's father who had come to

France earlier to fight the Iroquois. Her father was one of the **Carignan-Salières** *who came from La Rochelle, France in 1665 and built the fort at Chambly where we stayed.*

While Madame de la Rochelle was there she met and married her husband Charles who was also a son of an officer and a King's daughter. After they were married, they left Fort Chambly and moved to Montreal where they built the lovely house where the de la Rochelles now live. The Lieutenant still has to live at Fort Chambly because of the war and only comes home periodically. That is why they wanted to have someone stay with Madame de la Rochelle.

The first thing we did upon my arrival was to go to the market at the wharf to buy vegetables and fabric to make European style clothing for me. It seems my deerskin attire and hair style were not appropriate dress for living in Montreal! She even gave me a new pair of shoes, but they are not as nice as the beautiful ones that you made for me so many years ago. Madame de La Rochelle insists on paying for all of my new clothing and expects so little in return. I do some cooking and sewing and cleaning, but she is right there working alongside of me and chattering away as she is wont to do constantly! I don't mind as I love to have a woman's companionship.

She is of a very joyful nature and loves the Lord, our God, as much as we do. We attend Mass at the huge Catholic Church, the Church of Notre-Dame, which is the largest building I have ever seen! It is an extremely ornate building, very dramatic and imposing. Inside it is painted in colors of red, blue, purple, gold and silver and there are hundreds, yes, hundreds, of wooden carvings and statues! The ceilings are painted blue with gold stars. It is the most amazing site you could ever imagine, so different from our Meeting House at home or even the mission church at Lorette.

I thought perhaps there would be some French Huguenots here in Montreal but so far I have not seen any. Most of the Indians and other inhabitants have been converted to Catholicism just like in Quebec. How I would love to attend a simple Puritan meeting as we did at home! Perhaps someday we will be able to return to our beloved Deerfield. That is always my constant prayer, dear Ebenezer, as I know it is yours. In the meantime, we must be content to honor God where we are.

I am finding myself getting very sleepy as we spent the day traveling to the market and shopping.

Oh, I almost forgot the most important news! While we were shopping for fabric and other items for making my new clothing, you'll never guess who we saw! Reverend Williams! Yes, he had just come from another one of his attempts to see his daughter Eunice at Kahnawake and was at the market where he was meeting with Father Meriel. When I saw him I introduced him to Madame de La Rochelle and he said that he knows her husband Charles. He said that the lieutenant is a man of honor and that made me feel more comfortable living in his home.

After we chatted for a while, Madame de La Rochelle invited the two of them to dine with us that evening in her home. They accepted the invitation and while we were visiting after dinner, I asked Reverend Williams if he was intending to stop in Quebec on his way home to Deerfield. He said that not only was he stopping there, but he was planning on visiting you in Lorette while he was there. He thought that I was still there and had planned on seeing if we could be released, but he has since learned that the French government still will not pressure the Indians to release any more captives that are being held by them. It seems that we are the only ones from Deerfield that are still here that want to return home. All the others have been released or decided to remain here as French or Indian citizens. I think Joseph Kellogg may still be somewhere near Montreal, but I don't know if he has decided to stay or try to be released. Our friend Samuel Price is still in captivity, but I'm not sure where he is being held.

I asked Reverend Williams if he would stop by our house in the morning and collect this letter from me to deliver it to you and so I pray that if you are now reading this that you will soon send me a letter in return.

May God keep you in His care,

Your faithful friend,
Sarah Hoyt"

Sarah tucked the letter in the envelope and sealed it with the sealing wax which she heated from the candle on her desk. She then changed into her nightclothes, and saying a prayer, she snuggled down into the comfort of her bed, dreaming, strangely, not of Joseph as she had done in the past, but to her amazement, of Ebenezer.

Chapter Nineteen

"Brethren, I count not myself,
that I have attained to it, but one
thing I do: I forget that which
is behind, and endeavor myself
unto that which is before"

Philippians 3:13

S arah settled down into her new life in Montreal and tried to make peace with the fact that she may never again see her family or home again. She and Madame de La Rochelle busied themselves with making Sarah's new clothes. At first they used the yarn that they had purchased at the market in town to make garments for the approaching winter. Sarah spent many evenings in her room knitting warm mittens and other items to give to her mistress at Christmas.

One morning in early December, Lieutenant Charles de La Rochelle came home for Christmas and brought one of the soldiers from Fort Chambly who had no place to live while away from the fort. As he often did, the Lieutenant thought that his fellow soldier who had no family in New France would enjoy attending the festivities of the holiday season in Montreal.

After greeting his wife who was delighted to see him, he introduced her to Lieutenant Louis St. Germain.

"Lieutenant, may I present to you my beautiful wife Madame de La Rochelle. Her father was one of the "*The Carignan-Salières*" from France who came in 1665 and built Fort Chambly, and her mother was one of the *'filles du roi'*. We have engaged the services of an English captive to help my wife while I am at Fort Chambly. I understand that the lass is of great help to you, my dear?" Lieutenant de la Rochelle asked his wife.

Madame de La Rochelle nodded enthusiastically. "*Oiu, Mon Chéri!* Sarah is most agreeable and we do enjoy each other's company. She is teaching me many household skills that we enjoy doing together, and she sings!" she exclaimed. "She has a lovely voice and she has taught her many of the songs that she knows and I have taught her some of our French songs. I am pleased to make your acquaintance Lieutenant St. Germain. I trust that you and my husband had a safe and uneventful journey?

"*Oiu,* Madame," St. Germain said, then glancing over her shoulder, he saw Sarah entering the room with a basket of eggs that she had gathered for their breakfast. Noting her beauty, his face lit up with a most charming smile.

"Is this the English lass of whom you spoke?" he inquired as his eyes surveyed her form appreciatively.

"Oh, yes! May I introduce you to Sarah, my companion and friend. Sarah, please meet my husband Charles de La Rochelle and his fellow soldier from Ft. Chambly, Lieutenant Louis St. Germain."

Sarah curtsied in greeting, but St. Germain walked towards her took her palm in his hand, giving it a light brush with his lips. He looked into her deep green eyes which reflected the green brocade waistcoat she had put on to gather the eggs, and he thought that she would be a lass that he would like to get to know better, a *lot* better!

Sarah trembled at his familiar greeting and becoming flustered at his continued bold appraisal of her, turned away. "Perhaps I should go to the kitchen and prepare some breakfast while you and your husband catch up with each other," she said to Madame de La Rochelle. I will call you when it is ready," she said as she hurried out of the room.

She was surprised when St. Germain followed her into the kitchen.

"I thought that we should leave the Lieutenant and his wife alone since it has been many months since they have had the opportunity to be together," he commented when he saw her look of embarrassment and discomfort at his appearance. "Perhaps you would like some help in preparing the meal? I have learned to do some cooking and would like to assist you if you would allow me, Mademoiselle," he said as he grabbed a pot from the rack and went out back to bring in water for the eggs.

Sarah stood there, not knowing how to react to this stranger who had so completely shaken her.

When he returned, she placed the eggs in the water and went to the larder where she took out a loaf of bread that she had baked the day before. When the lieutenant left the room to put the eggs on the fire to boil, she placed a bit of jam and butter into a shallow bowl. When she started to cut the bread into slices, she was startled when St. Germain placed his hand over hers. "Allow me to do this for you, *Mon Chéri.*"

She demurred and let him cut the bread while she placed the china plates and silver on the table. *"What manner of man is this to be so familiar and to offer to do women's work?"* she wondered, then left him to check on the eggs. Again he followed her and brought the eggs in from the fire and placed them in a crock that he took off the shelf in the kitchen.

She invited Lieutenant and Madame de La Rochelle into the kitchen where they sat across from each other, leaving Sarah across from the intriguing Louis St. Germain. She wasn't sure, but she thought at one time during the awkward meal, she felt his foot brush against her ankle, but perhaps it was only her imagination or maybe an errant mouse had entered the house to get out of the cold.

After breakfast, Sarah told the rest of them that she would clean up while they visited in the living area. She hoped that St. Germain would follow her mistress and her husband, but was perplexed when he lingered behind.

"Lieutenant de La Rochelle has told me that he and his wife often are expected to host dinner parties, especially during the Christmas season. Do you dance, Mademoiselle?" he asked as he took her hand in his and spun her around. "I understand that all of their guests enjoy dancing at these parties and they have learned the latest dances from the continent.

Sarah pulled her hand away and stammered, "No, Lieutenant. I am a Puritan and we do not believe that the Lord wants us to participate in such worldly amusements!"

"Oh, but you are in New France now, *Mon Chéri*. You will be expected to act as a Frenchwoman. Perhaps you will allow me to teach you to dance so that you will know how to do so at their social events."

He again took her hand, bowed before her and turned her around in a gallant gesture. "Lieutenant de La Rochelle informed me that he is expected to hold a dinner and dance before Christmas and I would request that you accompany me. I will speak to Madame de La Rochelle and tell her of my intent," he exclaimed as he left her stunned and wondering what to make of his bold and much too brash assumptions.

She knew that her father and Reverend Williams would not approve of her attending such an event as a guest and definitely wouldn't condone her dancing. She wrestled with how she could avoid such an engagement and decided that she would talk to Madame de La Rochelle privately about her concerns when she could be alone with her mistress.

She spent the rest of the day praying silently and asking God to direct her, but could not avoid the attention of the handsome and persuasive Lieutenant Louis St. Germain.

After the midday meal, the men set out to do some errands in town and she was able to approach her mistress. Before she could share her concerns, however, Madame de La Rochelle burst forth with the announcement that she had talked to St. Germain earlier in the day and agreed with him that it would be a splendid idea for Sarah to accompany the bold lieutenant to their upcoming dinner and dance.

"How exciting it will be for you, Sarah!" she gushed. "You will finally be able to wear that beautiful silk gown that you made, the one that so pleasingly sets off your eyes and hair. You will look so lovely in it, *Mon Chéri!*"

Sarah had been uncomfortable even thinking about wearing silk because silk was forbidden in the English colonies. She remembered hearing the story of her neighbor Mary Stebbins who, as the town gossips often repeated, was presented to the county court and fined ten shillings for wearing silk, which was contrary to law. She had persisted in wearing it even though she had been presented to the court previously for the same offense. Sarah had hoped to avoid wearing the silk gown, but now she was confronted with a situation from which she felt there was no escape.

Sarah did not know how to reply and just stood there stunned at this announcement as Madame de La Rochelle forged ahead.

"I think that Charles St. Germain is quite taken with you and you will make the other young ladies of Montreal very jealous if you accompany him to this party. He is considered to be quite the catch, dear Sarah, and I am delighted that he has taken such an interest in you. Perhaps it will help you to forget about your former life and your friend at the Indian village and become an esteemed member of our society. King Louis XIV has been granting some of the officers nobility status and you could end up being a member of the French nobility!"

Sarah didn't even know how to respond, so she just nodded and asked if she could be excused to go to her room.

Madame de La Rochelle gave her assent and flitted off to make plans for her upcoming party.

Sarah plopped down on her bed and, shaking, sent up a prayer to God asking Him if it was truly His will for her to forget her former life and become a member of French society. She couldn't imagine that He would lead her on such a path and was confused as to what she should do. Lieutenant St. Germain was strikingly handsome and engaging with his deep brown eyes that when he looked at her penetrated so deep into her soul that she was frightened and excited at the same time. His dark, curly hair reminded her of Joseph's, but she wouldn't let her mind dwell on that.

In addition to those misgivings, Sarah wondered if the handsome lieutenant and Madame de la Rochelle's husband Charles had been among the soldiers who had raided her village and marched them into New France. She was confused and needed to talk to Ebenezer about her fears.

Seeing the parchment and quill on her writing desk, she decided to write another letter to Ebenezer, even though she didn't know how she would send it to him. Maybe just writing to him would help her clarify her thoughts and calm her anxieties.

Chapter Twenty

"Wherefore, be ye not unwise, but understand what the will of the Lord is."

Ephesians 6:17

Picking up the quill and parchment, she began,

Montreal, New France
December 1709

Dear Ebenezer,

I do not know if you received my first letter that I sent with Reverend Williams. I hope it arrived safely and that you are doing well and that your master Gassisowangen is treating you well.

I think of you so often and miss our times together, my dear friend.

I find that, even though Madame de La Rochelle treats me well and always has something to say, that most of our conversations are one-sided and rather shallow. She is preoccupied with fashion and parties and shopping. We do enjoy our times of music and that's a time when I feel most connected to her, but otherwise, I mostly just listen to her prattling.

Forgive me for saying that. I know it is a sin to talk about her that way, and I hope she never sees this letter, but

I did have to express my frustration at not being able to have a deeper conversation with someone like we used to do. I hope you know how very much I do miss that, and you, my dear friend.

It seems that Madame de La Rochelle will be hosting a dinner party in the next few weeks and she expects me to attend, not as her servant, but as a guest! There is a man, a Lieutenant named Louis St. Germain who is a fellow officer serving at Fort Chambly with Lieutenant de La Rochelle, that has asked for me to accompany him to this upcoming party and I have not been able to know how to respond to his persuasive advances, Ebenezer.

It is so foreign to the way we have been brought up to do such things, and I think that he desires to court me! What shall I do? He is handsome and dashing and all the young ladies in Montreal are after him, but he seems to want to pursue me, a simple Puritan girl caught up in a world not of my choosing. Madame de La Rochelle has insisted that I wear a new gown of silk that she instructed me to make for attending such social occasions! I do not know what to do about this as it is against our law to wear such frippery. How will I answer to Reverend Williams if he happens to see me dressed so extravagantly? I am caught between an obligation to obey my mistress as God instructs us to do and holding fast to our Puritan beliefs. The Lord tells us in Ephesians chapter six:

"Servants, be obedient unto them that are your masters, according to the flesh, with fear and trembling in singleness of your hearts, as unto Christ, not with service to the eye, as men pleasers, but as the servants of Christ, doing the will of God from the heart, with goodwill, serving the Lord, and not men."

I suppose that I will have to agree to the lieutenant's proposal so as not to insult the de La Rochelles and to be obedient to them as they are my masters, but St Germain wants to teach me to dance! Can you see me doing such a frivolous thing? Little did I know that I would be expected to live like a French woman when I left Lorette. I had just begun to accept the fact that I would have to live as a captive among the Hurons for the rest of my life when I was suddenly plunged into a whole new way of life. I am trying to adjust to the change and don't even know where all of this will lead, but you must know that I have not abandoned my Puritan beliefs or submitted to Father Meriel's constant demands that I convert to the popish way of worship with all its rituals and ornaments and such.

I do attend Mass as I am expected to do, however, just as we were in Lorette. I hope that you, too, are holding fast to the faith of our fathers, even though the pressure to convert is always with us. I find myself blocking out their observances and thinking upon some of Reverend Williams' sermons.

Do you remember when we were small children and he preached a sermon about Sarah Smith before she was executed? She had been tried and found guilty for the murder of her newborn child, born while her husband Martin was in captivity in Canada. We must have been about six years old then. We didn't understand that she had been violated at one time during his captivity, and then she took up with one of the soldiers that were sent here to protect our community and then she became pregnant from that relationship. She had the baby alone and when the baby died, she hid his body under her bed. She was charged with murdering her child by smothering him. Do you remember all of this?

I remember hearing that she was sent to jail in Springfield and a few months later her husband was released from captivity and came home. Two months later she was tried and convicted and a week later they hanged her! I think her husband Martin was one of the ones who was killed during the raid, as I think that his house was one of those we saw burning that day. I remember how Reverend Williams accused the whole community of being guilty for the fall of Sarah Smith and then said we were all guilty of our own sins. I will never forget that after he told of her many failings and sins, he said that according to our Puritan doctrine God's wrath would be lessened if she repented. Do you remember how shocked we all were when we looked over to see Sarah sleeping during the whole sermon and prayer?

Ever since then, I have been quick to repent of my sins and have always listened very attentively to our pastor's sermons and admonitions. I know that you have as well, Ebenezer. I hope that I will not have to do too much repenting while I am in Montreal! Please pray that whatever I do while living here will be pleasing unto the Lord.

One thing that is distressing me is that I think that Madame de la Rochelle's husband and Lieutenant St. Germain may have been involved in the raid on our village. I am so confused as to why the Lord has put me in this situation. Please pray that I will be able to endure this new life away from anyone who is dear to me.

I hear the men returning from errands and must go down and make preparations for the evening meal.

I will see if Father Meriel can deliver this letter or send it with one of the traders.

It is my prayer that you remain strong, and I promise to do the same, dear Ebenezer.

Your faithful friend,
Sarah Hoyt

p.s.
I pray that you will be able to send a letter as soon as you can. I miss you!"

The next time Sarah saw Father Meriel, he took her letter and brought her the first one that Ebenezer had written after she was taken so suddenly to Montreal. She was happy to receive his letter and hoped that all was well with him in Lorette.

Chapter Twenty One

—— ✥ ——

*"They speak deceitfully everyone with
his neighbor, flattering with their lips,
and speak with a double heart."*

Psalm 12:2

S arah felt very guilty as she slipped into the emerald green silk gown that she and Madame de La Rochelle had fashioned for her to wear to the extravagant social events that they were expected to attend. She just couldn't get over her feeling that she was not pleasing God by wearing such finery. She knelt by her bed and offered up a heartfelt prayer to the Lord and asked Him once again to show her His will.

When she didn't hear directly, she assumed that He would not disapprove of her being obedient to her master and mistress by attending the dinner and dance that would be held that evening at the home of Lieutenant and Madame de La Rochelle. Checking her reflection in the looking glass, she lifted one of her curls back into the intricately styled coif that Madame de La Rochelle had helped her do earlier that afternoon after they had made the final preparations for dinner.

Soon she heard Madame de La Rochelle's high pitched voice welcoming their first guests, and she quickly descended the stairs to offer her help in the festivities.

Sarah and Madame de La Rochelle had spent several days preparing the house for their guests with cooking and cleaning and moving furniture so that they would have plenty of room for dancing. Madame de La Rochelle had engaged the services of a French girl named Marie who was a welcome help to Sarah.

"Will Father Meriel be among the guests that you have invited?" Sarah had asked her mistress earlier that day as she polished the silver.

"No, he will not attend this evening's festivities. Like the other priests here in New France, he does not approve of the idea of dancing, but we do it anyway, yes? Previously I hired a dancing master to teach me the latest dances from Europe and when I told Father Meriel what I had done, he shook his head disapprovingly and disparaged the whole idea."

As Madame de La Rochelle set out a large bowl, filling it with brandy, Sarah asked, "Will the men be drinking from one large bowl rather than from individual tankards?" It seems a strange thing to me."

"Oh, yes, the soldiers and the trappers all drink from the same bowl together and do not hold back," she explained. After the dancing, we will leave them to their card playing and gambling and drinking and the ladies will retire to the drawing room to talk and perhaps sing and play some instruments. You, of course, will grace us with your beautiful singing voice. I am sure the ladies will enjoy this time together and we can teach them some of our English songs, *oui?*"

"Of course, Sarah agreed, but her thoughts were still on how she would manage the evening in the company of the daunting Lieutenant Louis St. Germain. With much trepidation over the forthcoming encounter with this man, Sarah continued with her labors as Madame de La Rochelle droned on and on in her excitement.

Now she could no longer avoid the engagement. The Lieutenant entered the room and immediately strode over to Sarah's side. He took her hand and kissed it as he bowed before her.

"Oh, *Mon Chéri!*" he whispered fervently. "Oh, but you are so delightful, so exquisite! Only God's creations can compare to the beauty that I see in you! My appreciation for your charms is infinite, without limits!" he said with flattering lips that disconcerted her. She backed away from his bold advances and suggested that they greet some of the other guests who were just arriving.

"Let Madame de La Rochelle care for the guests *Mon Chéri*, tonight is our night for pleasure, is it not?"

"I do not know how to respond, Lieutenant St. Germain! Your boldness causes me much confusion and chagrin. I fear that we do not share the same expectations for this evening's purposes. I am merely playing the hostess for Madame de La Rochelle and her husband as my duty to them. Please do not take my presence here as an indication of my interest in your intentions!" she said as she backed away trembling.

"Oh, but it is my understanding and expectation that you are to be my companion for this evening's festivities and I intend to be at your side, my beauty, for the entire night!"

Sarah felt a deep uneasiness in her spirit as he placed his hand familiarly on her back and led her to the dinner table where Madame de La Rochelle had announced that the meal was ready to serve. Sarah would have been much more comfortable taking the place of Marie who started bringing in the dishes of hot meat and vegetables and serving them to the guests.

All during the meal which seemed to go on for an interminably long time, Sarah did her best to avoid responding to

St. Germain's constant attempts at drawing her into conversation, often whispering what she considered to be improper comments that shouldn't be said unless you were betrothed. She dreaded the dancing that would soon take place and when it could not be delayed any longer, she fought back the desire to ask to be excused to go to her room. She knew that Madame de La Rochelle would disapprove, so she took a deep breath and suffered through the night's entertainment, which included dancing the *Minuet,* the *Bourrée, Canarie, Chaconne,* and *Gavotte*, all dances that the French in Europe were enjoying. Sarah stumbled through them awkwardly and was relieved when Madame de La Rochelle thanked the musicians and bid the ladies to join her in the parlor while the men set up tables for gambling and drinking.

Madame de La Rochelle caught Sarah as they were entering the parlor and asked her if she enjoyed her evening.

"It was fine," she answered. "I felt uncomfortable not knowing how to do any of the dances, but the Lieutenant was quite patient with me and taught me enough of the steps that I was able to survive."

"So you enjoyed the company of the handsome lieutenant?' she asked.

"It was fine, Madame", she demurred.

"Marguerite!"

"Marguerite," she answered as they joined the guests in the parlor where Madame de La Rochelle sat at the harpsichord and told her guests that she and Sarah would be sharing some of the English hymns and folksongs and hoped that they would enjoy them.

After about a little over an hour of enjoyable music, the women thanked their hostess and made preparations to depart. Their spouses joined them and everyone said their goodbyes.

After all had gone, Sarah made a quick trip outside to the necessary and was startled to see the flame of a pipe being lit in the shadows. Startled at seeing someone there, she turned to hurry back inside, but felt someone tugging at her arm.

"I thought you would never be finished with all of your music, *Mon Chéri!* I am so glad that you thought to seek me out as I have been waiting for you to finish our special evening!"

"No, Monsieur, I assure you that was not my intent. I was only attending to necessities before retiring," she protested.

"Oh, I think not, you little vixen!" he argued. "Come here, and let us continue where we left off, *oui?*"

"No!" Sarah said as she fled into the house, hearing his laughter echoing through the night. She dashed up the stairs, ignoring the questioning looks from the de La Rochelles and closed her door with a bang. With shattered breath, she fell to her knees, pleading for God to help her deal with this persistent man whom she knew to be all wrong for her.

When she finished her prayer, she went to her window to close the shutters. She heard someone giggling down below and peered out her window. There she saw someone who could have been Lieutenant St. Germain, taking the servant girl Marie in his arms and stealing a kiss. She couldn't tell if it was really the lieutenant in the darkness, so she closed the shutters and crept into her bed.

Chapter Twenty Two

—— ✑ ——

"Though he speak favorably, believe him not: for there are seven abominations in his heart."

Proverbs 26:25

The next morning, Sarah arose early to finish cleaning up after the previous night's party and was surprised to see the maid Marie still there. She was standing in the kitchen with her hair disheveled and the laces on her shift untied. When she saw Sarah, Marie hastily tied the strings on her shift and reached up to tidy her hair. Her cheeks were quite red and Sarah wondered if that was because she had been tending the fire. However when she looked at the fireplace, she saw that there was nothing left but a few coals from the night before.

"Oh, hello, Sarah," Marie stammered. "I didn't think anyone would be up this early. I must have fallen asleep after the party last night and am just getting ready to leave. *Bon Jour, Mademoiselle*, I will go now," she said as she hastily backed out the door.

Sarah bid her farewell, and, grabbing a basket and her cloak from the peg near the door, followed her out to gather eggs for breakfast. When she got outside, she heard Marie talking with a man behind the barn and assumed it must have been someone who had come to collect her and take her back to her home. His voice was familiar, but she didn't think too much about it as most Frenchmen sounded the same to her.

She waited until she no longer heard voices and then went to the chicken coop and gathered the eggs.

When she got back inside, she found the de La Rochelle's just coming down the stairs to start their day.

"Good morning, Sarah," Madame de La Rochelle greeted her. "It looked like you had a good time at the party last night with Lieutenant St. Germain. He didn't dance with any of the other ladies in attendance. You must feel very happy to have such a handsome man who is so taken with you!"

Sarah just nodded and changed the subject. "I have eggs and pastries and some leftover meat from the party for our breakfast. I also have some dried apples if you like. Please let me prepare the meal as you both must be very tired after hosting such a fine affair."

Lieutenant de La Rochelle thanked her and took his wife into the parlor where they talked about some of the people and happenings at the party. Sarah overheard Madame de La Rochelle discussing Lieutenant St. Germain. "Don't you think they make a fine couple?" she asked.

Sarah couldn't hear Lieutenant de La Rochelle's answer, but did hear his wife's response, "Really? Where did you hear that?" she said.

Sarah couldn't hear all the rest of the conversation, but she did hear the word "wife." She hoped they had gone on to gossip about other people who were in attendance the night before and that they were not talking about her and the Lieutenant getting married. She continued in her meal preparation and when she was finished, she called the La Rochelles into the kitchen to eat.

Neither one of them talked much with Sarah. She assumed they were just tired from the night before and so she quietly finished her meal and let her thoughts wander to the brash and overly assertive Lieutenant St. Germain. She didn't know how to tell him that she really wasn't interested in him, that her heart still longed for a closer relationship with her friend Ebenezer.

As she was cleaning up after the meal, she heard a horse coming up the lane and approaching the house. She stepped out the back door to see Father Meriel coming to visit.

"Greetings, Father. Please come in. The lieutenant and Madame de La Rochelle are in the parlor. Won't you let me take you to them?"

"Yes, Sarah, in a moment, but I have actually come to deliver a letter to you from Lorette. One of the fur traders brought it to me this morning."

He handed her the letter to read in private and left her to join the de La Rochelles in the parlor.

Sarah eagerly took the letter which she hoped was from Ebenezer and was delighted to see his familiar handwriting on the thick envelope. Tearing it open, she was pleased to see that he had included two letters dated separately.

She read the first one dated in October and blushed when she read his closing remark that said, "*Your friend and fellow captive who holds your heart captive in my hand.*"

She then she unfolded the second which was recently written and read,

> "*Lorette, New France*
> *December 1709*
>
> *Dear Sarah,*
>
> *I was so happy to receive your most recent letter. Father D' Avaugour*

delivered it to me this morning after he had received it from one of the trad-ers at the wharf while he was there to make some purchases. I received the first one last October when Reverend Williams was returning home from Kahnawake. I didn't have a way to get a letter delivered to you, but Father D' Avaugour said that if I hurried down to Quebec that I could talk to some of the traders there that are planning on making a trip to Montreal in the next day. I was able to get permission from Gassisowangen to make the trip and he agreed to accompany me as he wanted to sell some of our goods to the mer-chants there. So, if you received this, then you know that my attempts to send the letter were successful.

I am glad that you are adjusting to your new home, but, oh, Sarah, how I miss your smile, your voice and your company! How I would just love to sit and talk with you, sing with you, and pray with you!

You will think it strange, but I am becoming quite an expert with the bow! Gassisowangen has taken me on several hunting trips with the other men and, believe it or not, I, the world's worst marksman, have been successful at bringing back deer, elk, and even some rabbits! Gassisowangen often teases me about the first time he tried to let me shoot that rabbit on the way here after we were separated from the rest of our party. How embarrassed I was that we ended up not being able to find any other game and had to eat the wolf that you so bravely shot! Oh, Sarah, to this day I am so sorry that you had to go through that horrendous ordeal! You must have been so frightened! Gassisowangen says that he should have taken you hunting with them and left me to do the 'women's work'. To this day he often makes me work in the fields with the women as a reminder that I am not fit to be a man. Maybe now that I have become skilled with the bow, he will relent a bit and allow me to go on more hunts with the men.

By now you have probably already attended the holiday party that your new family put on. I can't imagine you wearing fancy French garments, Sarah, and silk? *I know that it must have been very difficult for you to decide to do this, but I think if you did, that God and Reverend Williams will understand. I certainly don't condemn you because I know that as it says in I Samuel in the holy scriptures that* 'God seeth not as man seeth: for man looketh on the outward appearance, but the Lord beholdeth the heart.' *I know your heart, dear Sarah, and I know that you are a virtuous woman who only wants to please our Lord.*

I hope that you were not too taken with this handsome Lieutenant St. Germain. I have to admit that I was a little jealous when I heard that you were going to accompany him to the party. Did you dance with him? I probably should not ask this. Forgive me, Sarah, for as I said before, I know your heart. Did you find out if he was one of the soldiers who attacked us? I can't even imagine the fears you must be experiencing. I have been praying that God will sustain you.

I continue to enjoy spending time with Hatironta and Kondiaronk,

Gassisowangen's daughters. They are growing so fast! Every time I see them, I realize that my own dear little sisters that perished in the fire would have been eleven and thirteen by now. It's hard to believe we have been here going on seven years and still no hope of being able to go home. I keep clinging to Psalm 37 verse 5 which says, 'Commit thy way unto the Lord, and trust in him, and he shall bring it to pass.'

Not only do I pray that we can return home someday, Sarah, if we continue to commit our way unto the Lord, but I pray that someday you and I will be together again.

With that thought, I pray that you have the same feeling and hope.

I remain faithfully yours,
Ebenezer

Chapter Twenty Three

❦

"Thou shalt not suffer a witch to live."

Exodus 22:18

Sarah wanted to write to Ebenezer, but Madame de La Rochelle sought her out to talk to her while the men visited in the parlor. Sarah began making some boiled pudding and started a stew made of meat and squash and beans for the dinner that she would most likely be serving to Father Meriel later on.

Madame de La Rochelle took a seat on a stool in the corner while Sarah continued with her preparations.

As she worked, Sarah's mind was churning with how she would ask if Madame de la Rochelle's husband and Lieutenant St. Germain were among the soldiers who raided her village and killed so many of her family and neighbors.

"Sarah, we have often heard of stories of witches in the colonies," Madame de la Rochelle asked, interrupting Sarah's thoughts. "Did you ever hear of any witches where you live?"

Ending any chances for Sarah to ask her questions that had been tormenting her, she said, "Well, there was one in our county a few years back."

"Oh, do tell me about her!" Madame de La Rochelle prodded enthusiastically. "Oh, I do love a good story!" she exclaimed.

"Well, it happened in the town just south of us by the name of Hadley," she began, abandoning any hope of sharing her concerns. "The woman's name was Mary Webster and her husband was quite a bit older than she," Sarah began. "It seems they became very poor and lived in a very small house. Sometimes the people of the town took pity on them and brought them food and other necessities as her elderly husband was not able to provide for her. She was an ill-tempered woman and would often speak harshly to her neighbors if she felt that they had in any way offended her."

"Oh, do go on!" Madame de La Rochelle pressed. "This is getting quite interesting!"

"Well, it seems that some of her neighbors grew quite abusive to her after her spitefulness towards them and began to call her a witch. Then people began telling stories of her, some probably made up or exaggerated, I think."

"What kinds of stories? I cannot wait to hear them!"

"Well, there was one account that said that when men were bringing their cattle by her house, which was on the street on the way to the meadow, she would put a curse on the cattle and horses so that they would stop in their tracks and run back towards the meadow from where they had just been led. The teamsters couldn't get their livestock to go by her house, and in anger they would barge right into her house and threaten to whip her. Some of them actually did whip her in their fear and frustration."

"Oh, my dear, this is quite fascinating! What happened to her?"

"There are other tales as well. Once she turned over a load of hay that a teamster was carrying near her house. When the man went inside to chastise her, she turned the load back again."

"Do you believe this really happened? Did anyone see it?"

"I don't know if it did or if the man was just making up stories to harm her," Sarah answered.

"Were there other stories?"

"Well, there is one that is most unusual. It was said that she once went inside someone's house and caused a babe lying in his cradle to be raised out of the cradle to the bedroom floor and back again three times with no one touching it!"

"This is very hard to believe!"

"Yes, and there's another story that at another house a hen came down the chimney and fell into a pot of boiling water and was scalded. Soon afterwards it was discovered that Mary Webster was suffering from a burn. After more such incidents, she was arrested and had to appear before the county court at Northampton. From there she was sent to Boston and put in jail until she could be further examined. There she went before Governor Bradstreet and Deputy Governor Danforth and nine others where she was indicted by the grand jury. The verdict was that she did not have the fear of God in her and was being influenced by the devil."

"What happened to her? Was she hanged?"

"They left her to further trial where she pleaded not guilty and said that she would be tried by God and the country. Then the jury found her not guilty."

"Not guilty? How surprising!"

"Well, the people of Hadley were very disappointed because they truly believed all the stories about her. Shortly after she was released, there was another incident that riled the people of her town. It seems that one of the deacons in the church, Phillip Smith, a man about fifty years old who was also a justice in the county court, a selectman, and lieutenant of the militia, a man not unlike my father, was murdered with what they say was hideous witchcraft. Mary Webster felt that he had treated her unjustly in some way or another, and was so threatening to him, that he was afraid of what she might do to him.

"Did she do anything to him?"

"A short time later he became very ill and weak and would cry out to the Lord, 'It is enough, it is more than thy servant can bear!' He claimed that she was casting spells and enchantments upon him. He told his brother to look after him and said that he would see strange things. 'There shall be a wonder in Hadley,' he said. 'I shall not be dead when it is thought that I am.'"

"Mercy!"

"Some of the young men in town were so upset at the woman when Mr. Smith kept repeating his charges that they decided to go to her house and cause disturbances towards her. While they were so occupied, Mr. Smith would finally be at ease and able to sleep peacefully. The young men did this three or four times and they were the only times that Mr. Smith was able to sleep."

"That sounds like a strong indication that she really was a witch, don't you think?" Madame de La Rochelle enthused.

"There's more," Sarah continued. "While he was ill in bed, pots of medicine which had been put out for him were mysteriously emptied. The people attending him would hear audible scratching sounds around his bed, and just to assure themselves that it was not the man himself making the noises, they would hold his hands and feet still. Sometimes fire would appear on his bed, but when those who beheld it began to discuss it, the fire would vanish. Sometimes other people would actually feel something moving in his bed not near where the man was lying. It appeared to be as big as a cat, but they could never catch it. Other times the bed would shake violently even though people would lean on the bed's head to try and keep it still.

"This is so frightening and bewildering to hear!" Madame de la Rochelle exclaimed, putting her hand to her heart.

"Yes, but it gets even stranger," Sarah went on. "Mr. Smith finally died and the people who viewed his corpse found swelling on one of his breasts, and several unexplained holes and bruises on his back. They pronounced him dead, but his countenance appeared as if he were alive. He looked more like he was simply asleep. He stayed that way from early Saturday morning until the Sabbath day afternoon. When they came to remove him from his bed on that bitterly cold day, he was still warm. On Monday, his face was like a mummy and was colored black and blue and blood was running down his cheek. Although no one else was in the room, chairs and stools were clattering noisily."

"What ever happened to this strange woman after all of this happened to that poor man?"

"Remember when I told you that several of the young men in town went to her and caused disturbances?"

"Yes."

"What they did was to drag her out of her house and hang her from a tree until she was almost dead. Then they'd let her down and do it again. Sometimes they would roll her in the snow and finally they buried her in it and left her to die."

"Well, that was a fitting end to her, was it not" Of course she died, didn't she?"

"No, and here is the strange part. The righteous man Deacon Smith died and Mrs. Webster survived to live another eleven years and died in peace at the age of seventy!"

"Well, there you have it! One just never can explain life's mysteries, can one?" Madame de La Rochelle reflected.

"Well, the Lord says in his word in Galatians 5:20-21 that

> *"Idolatry, witchcraft, hatred, debate, emulations, wrath, contentions, seditions, heresies, envy, murders, drunkenness, gluttony, and such like, whereof I tell you before, as I also have told you before, that they which do such things, shall not inherit the kingdom of God."*

"Then we'll just have to leave it to Him to judge, won't we?" Madame de La Rochelle said as she rose to help Sarah with dinner preparations.

Chapter Twenty Four

"Their feet turn to evil, and they make haste to shed innocent blood: their thoughts are wicked thoughts: desolation and destruction is in their paths."

Isaiah 59:7

The following March, Hum-isha-ma was frustrated that her plans to win over Ebenezer were not succeeding. She jealously watched him as he continued to spend time with his master Gassisowangen's daughters. She no longer had the prestige of belonging to Ashutuaa as the old woman had died that winter shortly after the first snowfall just as she had predicted. Now another woman of the tribe, Thaovenhosen's mother, had taken her place and Hum-isha-ma was seen as just another member of the Hurons.

She reasoned that if she were to have status in the village, she would have to find a way to become a member of Thaovenhosen's family. As she contemplated her options, she realized that the only way for her plans to succeed, would be to eliminate Gassisowangen and hope that Thaovenhosen would then adopt Ebenezer. If she could find a way to get rid of Gassisowangen's daughters who competed for Ebenezer's affections, then perhaps all of her dreams would come true. He would want to assuage his grief over the loss of his precious little Hatironta and Kondiaronk and would desire a wife who could give him children of his own. No matter what, she was determined that she would be that wife.

That evening as everyone lay down on their planks in the longhouse, Hum-isha-ma lay awake. As soon as she heard the rhythmic breathing of all the women, she slipped out of her bed and took a lighted log from the communal fire and left the dwelling. She crept across the way to the wigwam where Ebenezer, Gassisowangen and his family slept. She touched the burning log to the thatched roof that soon

A Captive Heart

caught fire and quickly enveloped the whole dwelling in flames. She threw the burning log behind the wigwam and then found Ebenezer choking from the smoke and trying to carry the girls out. Hum-isha-ma told him that she would take the girls away to safety. Ebenezer thanked her and tried to go back inside to rescue Gassisowangen and his wife, but was held back by a huge burst of flame. While he was thus occupied, Hum-isha-ma put her hands over the girls' faces and smothered them to death.

Ebenezer stumbled back behind the burning home and saw Hum-isha-ma shedding fake tears over his precious little adopted sisters.

"You must go and wake the people and tell them of this tragedy!" he shouted. "I will find Father D' Avaugour and have him help us take Hatironta and Kondiaronk to the mission church for now until we can bury them," he choked. "I don't know if Gassisowangen and his wife will have bodies left to bury. How did this terrible fire start? Do you know?"

"It must have been a spark from the fire," she answered as she left to wake the villagers to help put out the fire before it spread to other dwellings.

As Ebenezer ran to wake the priest, Hum-isha-ma went straight to the dwelling of Thaovenhosen. When she told him what had happened and that Ebenezer had escaped with only a few burns, he noticed that she had soot on her clothes and burn marks on her hand. He didn't question her as to why she was up during the night, but was somewhat curious. He immediately went to see what had happened and cried

221

out in grief when he saw the dead little girls lying in the snow behind the wigwam which was now just a smoking ruin.

He looked up to see Ebenezer followed by the priest who had hastily thrown his black robe on and was moving quickly towards the burned dwelling. He too grieved when he saw the bodies of young Hatironta and Kondiaronk.

"What shall we do with the bodies tonight?" Ebenezer asked as he let the tears flow freely. "It's just like what happened to my dear little sisters Mary, Mercy and Hittie," he mourned. "Why, Lord, did I survive and these precious little ones have to perish?" he lamented.

Father D' Avaugour placed his hand on Ebenezer's shoulder and comforted him, just as his own father would have done, and Thaovenhosen did the same.

"We will take the bodies of the little girls to the church tonight and talk about what to do next in the morning," the priest answered.

"Come with me, my son," offered Thaovenhosen. You may sleep in my wigwam and take the place of your friend Jonathan who is no more."

Ebenezer nodded and followed his new master into his home where he spent the night dreaming the same nightmares he had often had of burning houses and horrible screams.

Chapter Twenty Five

———— ⌘ ————

"Mine eye therefore is dim for grief,
and all my strength is like a shadow."

Job 17:7

The next morning Ebenezer was still grieving the loss of his dear Hatironta and Kondiaronk and also that of Mary, Mercy, and Hittie and the rest of his family who were now in Heaven. He left his fur-covered plank in Thaovenhosen's wigwam and went directly to the mission church as soon as he had dressed. On his way to the church, he ran into Hum-isha-ma who had been waiting outside his dwelling to speak to him.

"Ebenezer, are you going to see the priest this morning?" she asked as she walked beside him. "Do you want me to accompany you to see Father D' Avaugour in case he has questions for us about last night?"

"That would be fine," Ebenezer answered indifferently.

"Were you able to sleep?" she inquired as she grabbed his arm.

"Not very much. I grieved deeply for Hatironta and Kondiaronk and thought again of my own little sisters who were burned in our house in Deerfield when we were attacked."

Hum-isha-ma kept silent for several steps before she continued. "Do you not think that it is time that you marry and have children of your own?" she prodded. "It might help comfort you in your mourning. It is the tradition of our people to take captives to replace those whom we lost either in battle or in sickness. That is how I came to live with the Hurons when I was a child. Father D' Avaugour does not like that practice and would lead us to find other ways to mourn the death of a child. You should marry now and save the people from trying to take more captives to assuage their loss," she entreated.

Ebenezer thought of Sarah, but she was so far away and was in a place where she could have a warm bed and good food everyday and wear nice clothes and have the companionship of a mistress who held her in deep affection.

When they arrived at the church, Hum-isha-ma asked if she could talk to Father D' Avaugour alone for a few minutes. Ebenezer agreed and then went over to the place where the bodies of Hatironta and Kondiaronk were wrapped in skins and lying on a pallet on the floor. While he prayed for them and shed more tears in mourning, Hum-isha-ma talked to the priest.

"I think it is time that Ebenezer take a wife and have children of his own," she began after greeting Father D' Avaugour. "He misses his own little sisters as well as Hatironta and Kondiaronk and I would like to give him children of his own, if you will marry us," she proposed.

"He would have to agree to have the children baptized," Father D' Avaugour advised. "I do not think he would agree to be baptized himself and that remains to be a problem," he cautioned.

"Perhaps we could be married without his conversion," Hum-isha-ma suggested.

Father D' Avaugour stroked his beard thoughtfully and then responded. "I will allow him to marry, but only if he will agree to have any children baptized. That is my only restriction. Now, allow me to speak to Ebenezer privately." He dismissed her and she told Ebenezer that he could go in.

Father D' Avaugour saw the tears that still glistened in Ebenezer's eyes as he indicated a chair for him to use.

"I have talked with Hum-isha-ma and as is the custom among the Hurons, she has indicated to me that she wishes to be married to you to help comfort you in your grief. I am willing to perform the marriage and think that it is time for you to do this so you can produce children to take the place of your sisters for whom I can see you mourn deeply."

"But what about my refusal to convert to Catholicism?" Ebenezer questioned.

"I have considered this and, because of this recent tragedy, I am going to allow you to marry without converting, but only if you will agree to have any of the children you have to be baptized into the one true faith."

In his grief and because he was weakened from the lack of sleep the night before, Ebenezer nodded in agreement, but asked that he be allowed to tell his friend Sarah of the arrangement. The priest agreed and offered him parchment and a quill on which to write his letter. Ebenezer left the priest and went outside to compose this most difficult letter to Sarah, feeling that he had no other choice but to let things move forward.

Hum-isha-ma talked to the priest once more, and hearing that Ebenezer had agreed to her plan to marry, ran back to her home with glee.

Chapter Twenty Six

—— ✺ ——

"The Lord is near unto them that are of a contrite heart, and will save such as be afflicted in spirit."

Psalms 34:18

When Sarah finished her story about Mary Webster, the "Witch of Hadley," she thought that she would have an opportunity to ask Madame de la Rochelle about her husband and Lieutenant St. Germain's possible involvement in the raid on Deerfield, but Lieutenant de La Rochelle and Father Meriel entered the room before she had a chance to broach the subject which had been weighing so heavily on her heart.

"Lieutenant de La Rochelle tells me that his friend and mine Lieutenant St. Germain seems to be quite taken with you, Sarah. We have been discussing the two of you, and…"

"The *two* of us?" she interrupted. "Father, whatever are you saying?"

"As I was saying," he continued, "Lieutenant St. Germain is quite taken with you and he has indicated to Lieutenant de La Rochelle that he would like to be wed in the spring after he returns from a military campaign. As you have no father here to grant permission for the marriage, I have decided that Lieutenant de La Rochelle can speak as the one in authority over you and make the agreement for the marriage. It is time for you to produce children to populate our French colony and they will be baptized into the Catholic faith, even without your conversion," he declared.

Sarah was stunned at this announcement. "Have I no say in this matter? she asked.

"It has been decided," the priest said as he bid his farewell.

Sarah couldn't believe what she had just heard. She looked at Madame de La Rochelle and asked, "Did you know about this, Madame?"

"'Marguerite'," she corrected. "No, I did not, but I did see the way the Lieutenant attended to you and you only during last night's party. I do think that this is a good thing for you. However, I will miss your company if you leave Montreal with Lieutenant St. Germain. I understand that he may want to take you to live with him at Fort Chambly."

"But, I do not wish to marry this man!" Sarah objected.

"We women do not have any say in such matters," Madame de La Rochelle laughed. "But do not worry, my dear. You will learn to love him, I am sure. I cannot say that I had the same experience with my Charles. As you know, we met as children at Fort Chambly, my dear Sarah, and our parents arranged for our marriage. We have been quite happy. I am sure you will be the same with the handsome lieutenant. Now, let us continue with our labors. Perhaps you can teach me how to make candles, no?"

Feeling that she had no choice, Sarah agreed and they spent the day dipping candles and preparing meals. The day dragged on and Sarah only half listened to Madame de La Rochelle as she chatted about how they must make Sarah's wedding gown and other items for her to have as a new wife. All she could think about was getting some time alone where she could write to Ebenezer.

Finally after cleaning up the kitchen after the evening meal and making sure that she had everything ready for the following day's breakfast, Sarah excused herself and said that she was very tired from the previous day's events and wished to retire early. The de La Rochelles bid her goodnight and she went upstairs to write to Ebenezer.

She knew that her letter wouldn't be able to be delivered until the following spring when the snow melted, but she had to express her feelings to the one who she knew would understand.

She wrote:

> *"Montreal New France*
> *December 1709*
>
> *My Dearest Ebenezer,*
>
> *It is with great heaviness of heart that I write this letter to you as I fear it may be the last I will be able to write.*
>
> *You asked if I had danced with Lieutenant St. Germain. I fear that I had no choice. He was very insistent as were both Madame and Lieutenant de La Rochelle.*
>
> *Oh, but if that were only all that causes me such distress! I confess that I don't even have the words to tell you this latest development, but I will try as*

best I can with aching heart and shaking hands.

It seems that the man is quite taken with me and has asked for my hand in marriage! Lieutenant de La Rochelle has granted his permission as my master, and Father Meriel is not only pushing me to do this, but he is almost forcing me to do so. He insists that any children we have will be baptized as Catholics, but I refuse to convert!

I know that you are probably as distressed as I am about this news, but what am I to do? If only I were still with you in Lorette, my dear friend, I would request that Father D'Avaugour would allow us to marry! I don't know why we didn't do that when we had the chance. Perhaps you were afraid to ask or didn't think that I would consider such a move, but, I tell you this with all sincerity, Ebenezer. If I had known when we lived in Deerfield what a fine and honorable man you would become, I would never have agreed to marry Captain Alexander. I think that in my youth I was simply taken up with the glamour of it all because all of my friends were getting married. I had thought of you only as a dear friend back then, and now I have nothing but regret for what could have been.

Please know that I will never forget you, my dear Ebenezer, whatever the future holds. I pray that God will grant you peace and that someday you will be free to return home and perhaps marry one of the survivors or one of the released captives.

I know that you will not get this letter until the snow melts in the spring, so perhaps I will be a married woman by then and living at Ft. Chambly. Do you remember how well we were treated by the French woman when we were there? How wonderful it was to sit by a warm fire and have bread and other food to eat! That was another lifetime ago, when we thought that we would either be killed or redeemed, but neither has occurred.

I pray for your health and well-being. May God keep you in His care.

Your faithful friend,
Sarah"

Sarah slept clutching the letter to her heart. When she awoke, she placed the letter in the chest at the foot of her bed, and went downstairs to begin her day's labors.

That Sunday at Mass, Father Meriel announced that Lieutenant St. Germain and Sarah Hoyt would be wed in the spring when St. Germain returned to Montreal. Several of the unmarried young French women were shocked that the handsome lieutenant would be marrying a servant girl, although they had to see how he might have been attracted to her beauty.

Marie, the girl who had helped Madame de La Rochelle and Sarah at their dinner party, nudged a friend who was sitting next to her and whispered something in her ear. The other girl giggled and cast a condescending glance toward Sarah who was still in despair over the whole affair.

As they were leaving the church, several of the older women approached her and offered their felicitations, but she was puzzled when she saw some of the men cast knowing looks at each other.

Chapter Twenty Seven

"For they intended evil against thee, and imagined mischief, but they shall not prevail."

Psalms 21:11

As winter cast off its dreary pall, Sarah's mood did not improve. Even though the days grew longer and the sun was out more often, she felt a dark foreboding in her soul. She couldn't sleep, couldn't eat, and could hardly bear to listen to Madame de La Rochelle's incessant jabbering about her upcoming wedding. She had resigned herself to the fact that she would have to marry this man who could have been one of the soldiers who had wreaked so much evil and destruction on her village. She had given up talking to her mistress about her fears.

One early April morning Sarah and her mistress were eating bacon and eggs for breakfast and Madame de La Rochelle suddenly bolted from the table and emptied the contents of her stomach all over the kitchen floor. Fearing that she had a serious ailment, Sarah immediately went to her aid.

"Oh, Madame, I am so sorry! I did not know that you were ill!"

"Oh, no, I am not ill," she responded. "I believe that if all goes well, I am going to bring forth a new life at the end of the summer!"

"Oh, I am so delighted to hear this good news!" Sarah exclaimed as she wiped her mistress' face with a clean towel.

"I am very happy, but I only hope that nothing goes wrong with this one," Madame de La Rochelle explained. "You see, I have been with child many times and none of them have come to full term. The doctor has told me that I must rest or I may not only lose the babe, but my own life as well."

"Oh, I am so sorry to hear this. You must let me take you to your bed now," Sarah offered. "Does your husband know yet?"

"I sent a letter to him yesterday morning. My husband would want to come immediately, but I told him to wait until he comes next month. I will be fine until then if I just rest, but you know me. I am not one to just sit around. We have your wedding to prepare for! I am sure you are looking forward to being with your handsome lieutenant."

Sarah smiled weakly and changed the subject. "I will take care of all of the household duties from now on so that you can rest and prepare for your new babe."

"Oh, I almost forgot! I have engaged the services of the maid Marie who helped us during the Christmas festivities in December. She will be here in just a while to help you in your work so that I might do as the doctor says and rest."

"Would you like some help getting to your room?" Sarah offered.

"No, I will be fine," her mistress said as she rose to go upstairs.

Sarah then began cleaning the mess on the floor and when she was finished, she went outside to bring in water to take up to Madame de La Rochelle. When she opened the door, Marie was standing there.

"I have come at Madame de La Rochelle's bidding to assist you in your daily tasks," she said.

"Yes, I have been expecting you. Please come in and you can begin by cleaning the dishes from our breakfast while I make bread." Sarah couldn't help noticing that it looked like the maid might also be with child, but she said nothing.

As the two women were working, they suddenly heard a cry from Madame de La Rochelle. Sarah quickly wiped off her floured hands and bolted up the stairs to help. When she opened the door, she was met with the sight of her mistress covered in blood. Her face was deathly pale and she grasped her stomach and wailed, "Not another one," she moaned. "I fear this will be the death of me! Oh, Sarah, please get word to my husband and call for the doctor," she said weakly.

Sarah called for Marie. "Please fetch the doctor, Marie. I must stay with Madame de La Rochelle."

Marie agreed and left, but instead of going for the doctor, she went to the tavern where she worked in the evenings. When she entered, she saw Lieutenant St. Germain at the gambling table and quite drunk. When he spotted her he called her over, "Marie! Come here, my little flower and give me some sweetness!"

Marie sashayed over to St. Germaine and sat on his lap. He let his hand rove over her belly and asked, "What's this? Have you been eating too many pastries?"

"No, Lieutenant, I haven't. I think you know what this is! Do you not remember our little rendezvous in the barn last December at the de La Rochelles?"

"Oh, but of course! How could I ever forget?" he winked.

"But why did you ask that girl Sarah to be your wife? she admonished. 'You promised me that we would always be together."

"Oh, but we will *Mon Chéri*. You see, Lieutenant de La Rochelle lies dead at Fort Chambly from a wound in "battle", and he has written a will that states that should anything happen to him and his wife, that Sarah will inherit his property. No one knows that his wound came not from the enemy, but from the one who loves you, *Mon Chéri*."

"Oh, you are such a rogue!" Marie smiled. "I am now working for Madame de La Rochelle, thanks to your recommendation, Louis. She has just suffered a miscarriage and Sarah has sent me for the doctor. Should I do as she bid?"

"That will not be necessary, at least not speedily. Wait for an hour and then see if you can find the doctor. We will need him later. Lieutenant de La Rochelle has sent me here with the document for his wife to sign. They agreed to this when he was here in December and I overheard them talking about it when they thought me asleep. If you think she will survive long enough, I will go to the house and have Madame de La Rochelle sign the will and as soon as she does so, I will inform her of her husband's death and the shock of it just may be enough to kill her. If not, I have ways to assure that she doesn't survive. Then the doctor can come and confirm her death."

"But what about us and our baby? Marie asked, grasping her belly.

"Why do you think that I have asked Sarah to marry me? Don't you see, Marie? Once I am married to the wench, the property will be mine! Then we will see that something happens to her, and you and I will live like royalty in Montreal!"

With that, they each departed to their schemes, but little did Marie know that Lieutenant St. Germain's plans did not include her, no, not at all.

Chapter Twenty Eight

"A wicked man hardeneth his face: but the just, he will direct his way."

Proverbs 21:29

What the two conspirators did not know was that someone had overheard their plans. Reverend Williams was on his way back from Kahnawake where he'd had another unsuccessful attempt to see his daughter once again. He had just finished a meeting with the authorities in Montreal on behalf of the remaining captives. He had stopped in for a quick meal before going on to the de La Rochelles to deliver a letter from Ebenezer and to see if Sarah had any letters for him to carry on to Lorette. He was on his way to Quebec where he had planned to meet up with Reverend Stoddard from Northampton who was speaking to the authorities there regarding release of the captives. The two men had hoped to gain the release of all of the remaining captives, but as long as Queen Anne's War still raged, they had met with little success. He was hoping that Stoddard would have better success than he had.

He quickly paid the tavern owner for the meal and went to the livery stable for a horse to take him to warn Sarah, but was summoned by the voyageurs who were ready to leave, saying that he must come now or they would have to leave without him. With Reverend Stoddard waiting in Quebec, he had no choice but to leave with them, so he abandoned his plan to see Sarah and prayed that God would preserve her. He decided that he would get the news to Ebenezer and prayed that the young man would be able to get back to Sarah in time to stop the wedding. Before he left, he gave the boy at the livery stable a shilling to get a message to Sarah that she would be in danger should she marry St. Germain and asked him to deliver Ebenezer's letter.

The stable boy agreed and took off on his mission after receiving hasty directions from Reverend Williams. When he got there, he found Sarah weeping and a French officer striding away from the house grasping a sheaf of parchments. The officer rushed past the boy, rudely shoving him out of his way, and soon galloped away, leaving the bewildered boy to deliver the pastor's message and letter to Sarah.

"She's gone and so is Lieutenant de La Rochelle!" she sobbed. "What am I to do?"

"Do you mean the officer that just left?" the stable boy asked.

"No, I mean Madame de La Rochelle lies dead in her bed. We may have been able to save her, but she just received the most devastating news that her husband was killed in battle. It was too much for her in her weakened state and now I must talk to someone who can help. The man you saw, the French lieutenant, is on his way to the judge with the will that says that I am to inherit all of their property. He had Madame de La Rochelle sign it just before she died. It said that I must marry that lieutenant in order to do so."

"Oh, Mademoiselle, I am sorry. I have a message for you from the Englishman. He said you must not marry someone named Lieutenant St. Germain. He said it would be dangerous for you and gave me this letter."

"Thank you for delivering this message. Would you be so kind as to help me hitch up our wagon so that I may go to see Father Meriel with the news of Madame de La Rochelle?" she asked as she reached into the crock that held the money for her household expenses and handed him a coin.

"Of course, Mademoiselle, would you like for me to drive you there?"

"Oh, that would be very kind of you," Sarah accepted. She took off her apron that was still covered in Madame de La Rochelle's blood and washed her hands in the bucket of water that she was going to use to clean the kitchen before the tragic events that had happened so suddenly. By the time she had made herself presentable, the boy had finished hitching the horses to the wagon and was waiting to help her into her seat.

They hurried to the church and soon found Father Meriel in the garden tending to some plants. When he saw them coming at such a breakneck speed, he hastily went to meet them.

"Mademoiselle Sarah," he said as he helped her out of the wagon. "What is it, my dear? You look so alarmed. I hope you do not have bad news for me today," he inquired. "Perhaps you and your intended husband have had a little lovers' quarrel?" he teased.

"No, Father Meriel, it is not that but the most mortifying news that could be possible!"

"What is it, my child? Please come inside and you can tell me everything. Perhaps some refreshment will help you? I will ask the sister to bring us something," he offered.

"Yes, thank you, Father," Sarah said as he led her to a chair inside.

"Now tell me what has caused you such great distress. Are you having misgivings about your wedding next month? That is very common among young brides, my dear. I am sure you will see that all will be well."

"Yes, and no, Father Meriel, but let me explain the horrible tragedy that has befallen us."

"Please, proceed," he said as he took a seat across from her.

Sarah cleared her throat and wiped a tear from her eye and exclaimed, "Oh, Father, what are we to do? Madame de La Rochelle announced to me just this morning that she was going to have a baby at the end of the summer and…"

"Why, that is very good news!" Father Meriel exclaimed.

"No, Father, that is not all. Shortly after she told me this, I sent her up to her room to rest because the doctor had told her that he feared another pregnancy would be very dangerous for her and he ordered her to rest until the baby was born. After getting her settled into bed, I went back downstairs where the maid Marie was helping clean up. I noticed that she also seemed to be with child, but I didn't say anything."

"Yes," Father said frowning, "I suspected as much."

"Less than an hour after I put Madame de La Rochelle to bed, we heard a cry and I rushed upstairs to see what was the matter. I saw her lying in a pool of blood and called for Marie to run for the doctor while I tended her. She grew weaker and

I feared that she would not make it. She so wanted this baby after losing so many others. I could not stop the bleeding and she continued to weaken."

"Oh, I am so sorry," he said. "This is distressing news indeed. We must get word to her husband Charles.

"I kept hoping that Marie would come with the doctor, but instead, she brought Lieutenant St. Germain with her."

"Your lieutenant?" the priest asked.

Sarah didn't respond to his question, but went on, "He told me that he was on his way to bring the bad news to Madame de La Rochelle that her dear husband had been killed in battle. He made her sign a will that she and her husband had discussed doing when he was here last December. The will stated that should anything happen to the two of them, that unless they had children of their own, that I was to be their beneficiary and inherit their property. I do not care about the property, Father Meriel. I just wanted Madame de La Rochelle to live and have her baby, but just after she signed the document, she left her earthly body and went to join her husband in Heaven. I think it was the shock of hearing of her husband's death that killed her. I truly do," she moaned.

"Oh, my dear. This is most distressing news indeed. We must now make sure that you do marry Lieutenant St. Germain so that you do not have to be alone in that big house. You will need someone to take care of you."

"Father, I do not think it is proper for me to marry soon, if at all. I do not want to stay here in Montreal. I just want to go home. My mother is in Boston and I would really love to be reunited with her," she cried.

"My child, I do not believe that it will be possible for you to leave. If the will reads as you have stated, then you must stay and live in the home of the de La Rochelle's. That was their wish."

Sarah wiped her eyes and nodded, but then said, "Would it be possible for us to at least postpone the wedding so that I may have time to mourn the death of Madame and Lieutenant de La Rochelle?"

The priest said he would consider that and then the sister came in with their refreshments and they both sat in silence, each with their own thoughts, as they partook of the food and drink.

Chapter Twenty Nine

─────── ✑ ───────

*"Mine eye therefore is dim for grief,
and all my strength is like a shadow."*

Job 17:7

S arah and Father Meriel finished their refreshment and then left to return to the house to take Madame de La Rochelle's body to the church to await burial. Father Meriel followed in his own wagon which was driven by the undertaker who lived in a cottage on the church property. When they arrived, they found the doctor who was just getting ready to leave. He confirmed that the woman was dead and said the cause of her death was from bleeding and shock. The maid Marie was nowhere to be seen.

After the men left with the body, Sarah went to her room and opened the letter from Ebenezer which read:

> *"Lorette, New France*
> *March 4, 1710*
>
> *Dearest Sarah,*
>
> *My heart is breaking as I write this letter to you. Last night the most horrible tragedy happened. The wigwam of Gassisowangen where I slept with the family caught fire and he and his family were burned. I was the only one who was able to escape. I brought Hatironta and Kondiaronk out with me, but it was too late. They died from breathing all the smoke. All I could think of was my own little sisters Mary, Mercy,*

and Hittie and how they suffered in the same way. I loved those little girls as my own sisters and now I am bereft and even lonelier for you, my dearest friend, the one who holds my heart.

I am now living with Jonathan's master Thaovenhosen who has treated me with kindness, but has insisted that I take a wife and produce children for him. Father D'Avaugour wants me to marry Hum-isha-ma and I fear that unless I do, they will insist that I go on a raid to take captives to replace the ones who were killed in the fire.

He has permitted me to write to you and discuss the situation. What should I do, Sarah? You know that my heart is with you, but I could not allow myself to be the one to capture other innocent people like what happened to us and our friends and neighbors. Perhaps it is God's will for me to do as Thaovenhosen and the priest desire and for you to make a new life for yourself with the de La Rochelle family. I hope you won't marry that lieutenant that you met and danced with at Christmas, however. Perhaps you will remain unmarried, at least for now.

I hate the fact that we cannot be together as husband and wife, but it seems that God does not want it to be.

I must go to the market today with Thaovenhosen and sell our maple sugar. I will see if I can send this letter with one of the voyageurs that are there.

My heart longs for you and I pray that all is well. Perhaps by the time you receive this letter, I will be the husband of Hum-isha-ma.

God be with you, my dear Sarah,
Ebenezer"

Sarah read the letter over many times, believing that it would be the last one from Ebenezer once he took Hum-isha-ma as his wife. She knew that Ebenezer longed for a family of his own, and had wanted to be the one to give him children, but realized that it was not possible unless God sent a miracle.

She spent the night alone in the house, but stayed awake crying and praying to God for His will to be done. Towards morning she finally slept and was awakened by the pounding on the door downstairs. She hastily smoothed out her clothes that she had left on during the night and pulled her hair into her cap and ran down to see who was knocking so insistently.

Sarah unlatched the door to find Lieutenant St. Germain standing there impatiently.

"Why did you not answer the door when I first started knocking?" he demanded. "It is cold and blustery outside."

"I am sorry. I did not hear you at first. I had just fallen asleep after spending the night in mourning," Sarah explained. "It is not proper for you to come inside while I have no chaperone," she said, "but we can talk outside," she said as she grabbed her coat from the peg by the door.

"As I said, it is raining and quite chilly outside, *Mon Chéri,*" he objected. "Is it so wrong for me to be with the one who is to be my wife in just a few weeks?" he pressed as he pushed her back inside.

"No, Monsieur, I cannot allow such behavior."

"But, who will know?" he urged as he grabbed her and drew her close, kissing her fully on the lips.

"I will know and so will God!" she protested as she drew back smelling liquor on his breath.

"What does God have to do with it?" he said with disgust. "This is between you and me, my lovely bride to be."

Sarah wiped her mouth and continued to pull away until she ended up with her back against the kitchen counter.

"Oh, I see that you will not be easy to tame!" he laughed. "Very well, *Mon Chéri,* I will leave you for now, but remember, you will not always be able to avoid my advances once we are married!" he chided her as he strode away.

Sarah stood there shaking after she bolted the door and then slumped down onto the floor where she remained for over an hour crying and praying until she had no more strength and fell asleep on the floor.

Chapter Thirty

"Deliver me, O my God, out of the hand of the wicked: out of the hand of the evil and cruel man."

Psalms 71:4

Reverend Williams prayed the whole way to Quebec and told the voyageurs that he would forgo an extended time in Trois-Rivières as he needed to get to Quebec as soon as possible with an urgent message for one of the men at Lorette. As they were also in a hurry to get to Quebec, they obliged him by spending just a few hours in Trois-Rivières where they traded some goods and gathered supplies for the rest of their journey.

When he arrived in Quebec, he hired a horse to take him to Lorette and raced to the village to warn Ebenezer of Sarah's danger. When he arrived, he found the young man in the field practicing with his bow and arrow.

"Reverend Williams! How good to see you," Ebenezer said as he put down his bow. "What brings you to Lorette? Do you have news of Sarah, a letter perhaps?"

'I am afraid that I do not have a letter for you this time, but an urgent message," he responded.

"Please come and sit on this log and tell me," Ebenezer said, his heart constricting with fear. "Is it about Sarah? Is she alright?" he asked.

"For now she is, but I fear that she will not be for long," he answered."

Ebenezer's hands gripped the edge of the log and his fingernails dug into the rough bark. "What is it, Reverend?"

"Lieutenant and Madame de La Rochelle are both dead. He was supposedly killed in battle and she may have died from a miscarriage and the shock of finding out about her husband's death. While in the tavern at the wharf where I was taking a meal before going to see her and deliver your last letter and see if she had one for you to send with me, I overheard Lieutenant St. Germain talking with a tavern wench about his plan to steal the property of the de La Rochelles. He admitted to killing Lieutenant de La Rochelle while they were on a military raid and claimed that he was killed by the enemy."

"This is the one that Father Meriel wants Sarah to marry?" Ebenezer gasped.

"The very one, but there is more to this tragic story. It seems that when Lieutenant de La Rochelle was at his home in December, Madame de La Rochelle requested that Sarah be the beneficiary of their property should anything happen to the two of them, unless, of course, they had an heir."

"Really? That was most thoughtful and generous of them to esteem her so highly."

"Yes, Madame de La Rochelle grew to love her like a sister. But, to continue. It seems that Lieutenant St. Germain overheard them discussing their will when he was staying with them for the holidays. He then decided that he could gain title to their property if he could persuade Sarah to marry him. Once married, then he would be the rightful owner of the property as the husband always is. He told the tavern maid, who was carrying his child, by the way, that he would see that once he was the owner of the property that he would see that something would happen to Sarah that would leave him free to marry the wench."

Ebenezer jumped up from the log and paced back and forth saying, "I must go to her and rescue her from this abomination! Does she know about this evil that has befallen her? Were you able to see her and warn her?"

"I was not able to go to her as the voyageurs were anxious to leave. I sent word with a stable boy who also took your letter with him. All I had time to tell him was that she must not marry this man, that he was dangerous. We can only pray that God will keep her safe and that the marriage will not take place. Father Meriel has been insistent that she marry him, so I hope that you can get to her and save her from this treachery. While on our journey, I also learned that Lieutenant St. Germain's mother was one of the "King's Daughters", but when she was abandoned by her husband because she refused to do manual farm labor, she turned to a life of prostitution. St. Germain is one of her illegitimate children. He became a soldier when he grew up because he heard that King Louis was granting nobility to some of the soldiers. He is a very ambitious man who will stop at nothing for gain, including murder and deception."

"Reverend, let us pray that Thaovenhosen will allow me to go to Sarah and save her from this wicked man. I cannot bear to think of the harm that will come to her as part of his evil schemes."

"I will pray, my son. Now you go to Thaovenhosen and I will go to Father D' Avaugour and tell him all that has transpired and how we must act quickly to save Sarah from this treachery."

The two then said a quick prayer and went their separate ways. Ebenezer found Thaovenhosen in his wigwam in deep discussion with his wife Sah-teenk-kah, whose name meant *"Magic Dancer."* When he approached the wigwam, he stood outside the dwelling and waited until they were done speaking. He was surprised to hear Sah-teenk-kah tell her husband that while outside taking care of personal needs, she had seen Hum-isha-ma walking towards the wigwam of Gassisowangen with a burning log in her hands the night of the tragic fire.

"Why did you not say anything before this?" Thaovenhosen admonished her. "Would you have her go unpunished for this evil deed? Are you sure it was Hum-isha-ma?"

"I am almost certain, but I didn't know what her motive was until I saw that she was pressuring Ebenezer to marry her. You know that he would not want to participate in taking captives to replace the girls. You gave him the choice of either that or marrying Hum-isha-ma and I thought it would be better for him to marry than to be forced to take part in a Mourning War. I have prayed to Jesus and feel that we must let him know that he does not have to marry her or take part in a Mourning War."

Thaovenhosen grunted and said, "Perhaps you are right. I will talk to the young man and also to Father D' Avaugour," he said as he arose.

Ebenezer waited until Thaovenhosen came out of the wigwam and asked if he could talk to him. Thaovenhosen assented and Ebenezer told him what Reverend Williams had said. He was just about to ask for Thaovenhosen's permission to go to Sarah when the Indian said, "Sah-teenk-kah has just given me some troublesome news regarding Hum-isha-ma and I must talk to Father D'Avaugour about it. Come with me, Ebenezer, and we will talk to him."

"Reverend Williams is talking to him now about what he discovered in Montreal."

"You must know that you no longer will be bound to marry Hum-isha-ma, Ebenezer."

"Why is that?"

"Sah-teenk-kah told me that she saw Hum-isha-ma with a burning log approach the home of Gassisowangen the night of the fire. We believe that she is responsible for that tragedy."

"But why would she do such a horrific act?" Ebenezer asked.

"We do not know. That is why we must talk to Father D' Avaugour right now," said as he strode towards the mission church with Ebenezer following quickly behind.

"When they entered the church, they found Reverend Williams and Father D' Avaugour in prayer and waited until they were finished before approaching them with their news.

"What is it, my friends," Father D' Avaugour asked when he saw the two men. "Did you want to talk about what to do about Sarah Hoyt? Reverend Williams has just told me of his deep concern over her welfare and has asked permission for you to go to her. I feel that I cannot grant that permission, but must leave it to your master Thaovenhosen to approve of this. Remember, you are to marry Hum-isha-ma this next week and should not leave her to go after another woman," he cautioned.

"That is why we have come to talk to you, Father," Thaovenhosen explained. "My wife Sah-teenk-kah has just told me that she saw Hum-isha-ma approaching the dwelling of Gassisowangen the night of the fire and thinks that she was responsible for starting the fire."

"This is very distressing to hear. Are you sure?" the priest asked.

"We are sure," Thaovenhosen assured him. "We think that she wanted to find a way to force Ebenezer to take her as his wife. She has long desired to marry him, as you know, and perhaps she thought this would be a way to ensure that her wishes were met. When we gave Ebenezer the choice of going on a raid to take captives to replace the girls who died or to marry and have children of his own, he agreed to marry Hum-isha-ma. Now that we have learned what she did and what treachery is facing Sarah Hoyt, I would like to ask for your permission to call off the wedding and determine a punishment for Hum-isha-ma. Then I would like to go with Ebenezer to Montreal to bring Sarah back to our village where they could be married and raise children for us. Ebenezer has agreed that they will allow any of their children to be baptized as Catholics if you will allow us to go for her."

"I think that is a good plan," Father D'Avaugour agreed as he looked to Ebenezer. "Are you in agreement that if I allow this, that you will let us baptize you children as Catholics and live with us in Lorette?"

All Ebenezer could think about was his concern about Sarah and her safety, so he quickly agreed.

Ebenezer bid Reverend Williams farewell and left with Thaovenhosen to gather food and supplies for a journey to Montreal. Thaovenhosen told him to bring his bow and arrow so they could hunt for meat on their journey and Ebenezer went back to the place where he had left it when he first learned about Sarah's situation from Reverend Williams.

Soon they were on their way in one of the canoes that Ebenezer had helped to make earlier that year. He was thankful that Thaovenhosen was willing to go with him to rescue Sarah. He wasn't sure that Gassisowangen would have done the same.

The men travelled as fast as they could against the current, but it took more than a week to travel the two hundred miles between the two cities. When they arrived in Montreal late one morning, they were exhausted and hungry so they went first to the tavern at the wharf where they traded some maple sugar for a meal. When they had hastily finished eating, they asked the tavern owner if he knew how to reach the house of Lieutenant and Madame de La Rochelle.

"Are you here for the wedding of the English girl to Lieutenant St. Germain?" the man asked.

"No, we are here to stop it!" Ebenezer responded.

Lieutenant St. Germain, who was sitting in the darkness finishing what must have been one of many drinks, jumped out of his seat, knocking over the table as he angrily confronted Ebenezer.

"Who are you and what right have you to stop my wedding, you scrawny little savage!"

Thaovenhosen strode over to the lieutenant and stared directly into his eyes, saying nothing.

When Ebenezer saw St. Germain, his heart almost stopped when he recognized him as the man who had shot his father and brother Henry. He shook with fear and rage as he lunged for the man.

"We know what evil schemes you have planned for her and we are here to see that they will not be accomplished!" Ebenezer challenged. "Furthermore I know that you were the one who murdered my father and brother!" he choked.

"Go away, you little savage. Go back to your village and leave me be," he shouted as he brushed Ebenezer aside. "If you think you can fight me, an officer in the king's army, then let us fight for the wench." he challenged.

"Are you challenging me to a duel?" Ebenezer responded.

"Yes, I am, if you think you are man enough to fight!" St. Germain sneered.

"If it means saving Sarah from the likes of you, then, yes, I will fight for her and also avenge the deaths of my father and brother!"

"Choose your weapon, mouse, but be warned, "I will fight to the death to marry the wench. I have plans for her that you cannot understand. You probably can't even shoot a pistol or use a sword, so this should be quite amusing," he slurred.

Ebenezer looked to Thaovenhosen who pointed to Ebenezer's bow and arrow. "I choose the bow, but you may use whichever weapon you choose," Ebenezer responded.

"Fool!" St. Germain jeered. "Let us go outside and get this little spat over with."

They left the tavern followed by several of the men who were placing bets and laughing. Several were pretending to shoot a bow and arrow and falling down in jest.

Ebenezer and Thaovenhosen walked away from the men and said a prayer asking for God to help Ebenezer.

Lieutenant St. Germain chose the tavern owner as his second and a dueling pistol for his weapon. Thaovenhosen placed the bow and arrow in Ebenezer's shaking hand and repeated the verse from Isaiah 41:13 that Ebenezer had shared with him on the journey to Montreal which said,

> *"For I the Lord thy God will hold thy right hand, saying unto thee, Fear not, I will help thee."*

The verse steadied his hand and Ebenezer strode over to St. Germain. The two men faced off with each other and the taunts and mocking laughter from the men grew louder and more boisterous. Finally the tavern owner gave the signal. Time seemed to stop and the voices of the men sounded like they were coming from underwater. Ebenezer lifted his bow, carefully placed his arrow in the string as he had been taught, and thought of the rabbit that he had missed while on the march north to New France. He vowed that this time, with the Lord's help, he would hit his target.

St. Germain sneered as he placed his finger on the trigger. Just as he was ready to pull it, the pistol was jerked out of his hand. He looked down to see the arrow protruding from his hand, which was now searing with pain. He looked in shock at Ebenezer as the crowd grew silent. The tavern owner picked up the lieutenant's pistol which never had a chance to fire, and led St. Germain into the tavern to try and remove the arrow.

"This is not over, savage!" St. Germaine shouted, as he cursed Ebenezer. "I will prevail!" The onlookers wandered back into the tavern, avoiding looking at the lieutenant, who was cursing and howling in pain as the tavern owner grasped the arrow and started pulling it out.

"You fool!" St. Germain bellowed. "Cut off the ends before you pull it out! Do I have to do it myself? Hand me my knife if you are so stupid!"

The tavern owner took the knife and cut off the tip of the arrow and pulled it out. Just then the maid Marie appeared and saw St. Germaine screaming and cursing as the tavern owner poured ale on his wound. She saw what was going on and quickly ripped her petticoat and made a bandage for his hand. Then she led him upstairs where she continued to care for him.

"Lieutenant, your wedding takes place in a just few hours, but first lie down and calm yourself. You must not let this little incident stop our plans. Come now, let me comfort you."

Chapter Thirty One

"The Lord is my light and my salvation, whom shall I fear? the Lord is the strength of my life, of whom shall I be afraid?"

Psalms 27:1

S arah finished cleaning up after her breakfast which she had been unable to eat because she was so distraught over her marriage that was to take place later in the day. She had hoped to avoid it, but Father Meriel was insisting that it would be the best option for her now that the de la Rochelles were dead.

"You cannot live in that big house by yourself, my dear," Father Meriel had told her when she had gone to him the day before pleading that he would call off the wedding. "But, don't you see? Lieutenant St. Germain has been transferred to the fort here in Montreal. He will be able to be home with you most of the time, unlike the situation with Lieutenant and Madame de La Rochelle who were a day's journey away and were unable to see each other except very infrequently. A little pre-wedding jitters is very normal. You will find that you will get used to being a wife, especially when you can live in style in one of the finest houses in Montreal. Now, you go back to that fine house and prepare for your wedding tomorrow afternoon," he said in dismissal.

It seemed that the whole town had been invited to the wedding. Many were curious to see the dashing young officer who would be marrying a captive English girl, and the gossips were having a hey-day.

Sarah watched the carriages pass by her window heading for the church and knew that too soon one of them would be stopping by her home to take her to the Church of Notre-Dame for the wedding. Facing the inevitability of her destiny to marry St. Germain, she went up to her room and took the wedding gown out of the chest where she and Madame de La Rochelle had placed it, and gathered up the rest of the items she would need as a bride. How she wished that she could be marrying for love to a man that she respected and honored, but, sadly, it was not to be.

She tenderly picked up her precious Bible and sat reading from her favorite book, the Psalms, and found verse 71:12 that after reading it she prayed:

> *"Go not far from me, O God: my*
> *God haste thee to help me."*

Although she didn't know it when she prayed, help was on the way.

She took her clothing downstairs to await her driver to the church. Soon she saw a fine carriage stop and one of the sisters of the Congregation de Notre-Dame alight to help take her to the church where in just an hour she would have to go through with the wedding ceremony. She followed the sister into the carriage and went forth to meet her destiny.

When they arrived at the church, the sister led her into a small room where she could change into her wedding attire. The sister helped her dress and then left her to her own thoughts while she waited to be led into the chapel. Sarah read from her Bible and then paced back and forth fervently praying that God would provide a way for her to be released from this duty that she dreaded. She had seen a side of Lieutenant St. Germain that the de La Rochelles and Father Meriel had not observed, and she was frightened about what kind of life she would lead once she was married to him.

She could hear people starting to enter the chapel and music beginning to play and knew that there would be no escape. Before she knew it, the sister came back and told her that it was time. She led Sarah down a long hallway which opened to a room at the entrance to the church. She wished that her father or even Reverend Williams could be there to walk her down the aisle, but the only one there was one of the priests.

As the doors opened and the music grew louder, she held fast to her Bible and looked towards the altar at the front of the church. There she saw Father Meriel dressed in white robes and wearing a large silver cross around his neck. Next to him was Louis St. Germain, her intended husband, smiling greedily at her. She noticed that he was a bit pale and his right hand was wrapped in bandages. Knowing his temper and his love of strong drink, she imagined that he had probably been in some kind of fight before coming to the church.

She thought back to her days in Deerfield where as a child, she and Ebenezer would spend time singing and sharing Bible verses after school. She remembered her dreams of becoming a wife and raising a family in the dear town where so many of her friends and relatives lived. She let her mind recall the talks that she and Ebenezer had back in the Huron village and her mind filled with regret that they had not joined as husband and wife, even if it meant that they would have to abandon the faith of their upbringing and raise their children as Catholics. Wouldn't the Lord have understood? But she knew now that all of that was in her past and that she must submit to a life not of her choosing. She said farewell to that other life and looked towards the man waiting there for her, not with a look of love as she had seen from Ebenezer, but of possessiveness. She swallowed and tried to calm her apprehensiveness.

As she slowly walked toward the altar, the doors behind her suddenly burst open. Several people turned around to see who would be so bold as to make such a commotion. Several of them gasped and started to murmur. Sarah looked up to see St. Germain's previously pale face suddenly turn red in rage. She turned around to see who was causing such a reaction and was stunned to see Ebenezer and Thaovenhosen, dirty and sweaty approaching her.

Father Meriel shouted at the intruders. "What is this? You must leave at once!" he commanded. "Someone remove these despicable savages so that we may proceed with this wedding! Miss Hoyt, come forth at once and say your vows to your intended husband. This is a travesty and I will not stand for it!"

Sarah turned around and smiled at Ebenezer and Thaovenhosen and then declared, "Father Meriel, I believe in marriage, and I truly desire to produce children, and I will even allow them to be baptized into the Catholic faith, but

I will not marry this man who stands beside you. I will only marry one of the captives, if any will have me!"

The onlookers gasped in surprise and were shocked that she would give up the opportunity to marry the handsome young officer. Lieutenant St. Germain leapt from the altar and bolted down the aisle and grabbed Sarah by the arm and started dragging her to the altar. "You will come with me right now!" he hissed as he pulled on her arm.

Father Meriel called out, "Stop this at once! There is no need for this dire behavior! There are no captives here, just these two coarse savages who have burst into this ceremony uninvited."

He was interrupted by Ebenezer's loud proclamation, "Sarah Hoyt! I, Ebenezer Nims, request your hand in marriage this very day, if you will give me the honor of becoming my wife!"

Sarah immediately pulled herself loose from St. Germain's grasp and fled to Ebenezer where all she could do was run to his open arms and cry.

He took her into his arms and whispered, "I should have asked you all those years ago when we were back home, but I was too shy and didn't think you would accept my proposal. I was just about to ask you when I brought you your new shoes, but your father, whom I always somewhat feared because he was a leader of the town militia and a deacon, answered the door. Then he told me that you had just agreed to marry Captain Alexander and I left in despair."

"Wasn't that the same day that your brothers were captured?" Sarah asked.

"Yes, it was, and other than the day that our whole town was attacked, it was the worst day of my life," he answered.

"I now believe that I would have said 'yes' if you'd asked me to marry you," Sarah admitted, but you never did.

The two were totally oblivious to the reactions of the onlookers and continued on with their conversation. Finally, Ebenezer leaned back and with eyes shining, he placed a tender kiss on her lips and held her close. She looked up at him and with all the love in her heart said, "Oh, Ebenezer, if the priest will agree, I will marry you this minute!"

Ebenezer kissed her again, much more deeply this time and Sarah returned his kiss with fervor.

Father Meriel was astonished to see that the man he thought was an Indian because of his dress was actually an English captive. Watching the two of them, he finally gave in to the wishes of the two young lovers. "I will agree to marry you two English people on the condition that your children will become citizens of New France and be baptized into the Catholic faith."

The couple nodded their assent and St. Germaine stormed out of the church, cursing under his breath.

Father Meriel then proceeded to marry Ebenezer and Sarah. They left the church on one of the horses that Ebenezer and Thaovenhosen had procured from the stable boy at the wharf.

"Shall we go to the house first to gather your things?" Ebenezer asked.

"No, I don't think it wise," Sarah cautioned. Lieutenant St. Germain will probably be there waiting to cause us harm."

So, they headed to the wharf instead, and after quickly returning the horse and buying some supplies for their journey, they rushed straight to the canoe that the men had hidden a ways down from the market area. As they drifted down the river back to Quebec and Lorette, Ebenezer held Sarah and whispered in her ear, Proverbs 18:22

> *"He that findeth a wife, findeth a good thing, and receiveth favor of the Lord."*

Sarah smiled and answered, "Yes, and she who finds a husband, finds a good thing, and receives favor from the Lord too!"

Then Ebenezer teased her with verse 7:11 from Song of Solomon,

> *"Come my well-beloved, let us go forth into the field: let us remain in the villages."*

They kissed again and held fast to one another.

They laughed and Thaovenhosen smiled as he continued paddling.

Chapter Thirty Two

***

*"Who shall find a virtuous woman?
for her price is far above the pearls."*

Proverbs 31:10

The three finally reached Quebec after several days of travel. After sitting for so many days in the canoe, they were happy to walk the eight miles to Lorette. When they arrived, they were greeted with smiles and shouts of glee. The Hurons welcomed Sarah as one of their own, and led the couple to their new home which they had constructed for them in faith that the quest to save Sarah would be successful.

As they passed the spot where Gassisowangen's wigwam had burned, they stopped and said a prayer for the little girls who had been like family to Ebenezer.

"I know how much you miss them and also your own little sisters, Ebenezer, but now we must pray that God will give us children of our own to love."

"And, I am anxious to get started on doing our part to make sure that happens!" he winked as he grabbed her hand.

Sarah blushed as he led her to their wigwam where they would live as man and wife, and if God so granted, as parents someday. Outside their dwelling, they were not even aware of the celebrations that were occurring just outside their door.

The next morning they were greeted with knowing smiles and some of the women patted Sarah's belly. Father D' Avaugour welcomed them and asked about their adventure. After they shared all the happenings, Sarah asked if she could have parchment and ink so she could write a letter to Father Meriel thanking him for allowing her to marry Ebenezer. She also wanted to let him know that it was her wish to will the home of the de La Rochelles to the sisters of the Congregation de Notre-Dame to use as a home for unwed mothers. She thought of the maid Marie and others who had been led astray by men like Lieutenant St. Germain and prayed that they would receive help from the sisters and would come to know God's forgiveness and mercy.

Ebenezer and Sarah had hoped that they would soon have children, but each month, they were disappointed when Sarah's courses began. They prayed each day that God would give them the child they wanted so badly, but He didn't grant their requests until one morning in May of 1712 while Ebenezer and Thaovenhosen were at the river fishing, Thaovenhosen told him that he had had a dream the night before where God had told him to give Ebenezer the following promise from Genesis 18:14:

> ***"Shall anything be hard to the Lord? at the time appointed will I return unto thee, even according to the time of life, and Sarah shall have a son."***

Ebenezer choked back a tear and said, "Truly, you speak the Lord's word. I must tell Sarah."

Thaovenhosen smiled and nodded and said, "Go, Son, give her this promise from our Lord."

The next February on St. Valentine's Day, Sarah brought forth a son and named him Ebenezer after his father. His name meant "*hither by Thy help I'm come*" and was a commemoration of divine assistance in the Bible. Sarah and

Ebenezer were delighted, as were Thaovenhosen and his wife Sah-teenk-kah who considered the baby to be their own grandchild.

One who was not happy with the birth, however, was Hum-isha-ma. Since she had been found guilty of starting the fire that killed Gassisowangen and his family, she had been ostracized from the people of Lorette and was confined in a room at the mission while awaiting a most probable death by hanging.

Sarah knew that Hum-isha-ma carried a great hatred towards her and she wanted to talk to the woman before she was executed. She asked Father D' Avaugour if she could speak to the woman before she died and he granted her permission.

"What do you want with me?" Hum-isha-ma spat out when she saw Sarah enter carrying her baby on her back. "If not for you, I would not have had to take the lives of Gassisowangen and his family. Ebenezer would not consider me for marriage and I had to do what I did to make him marry me! Now I will go to hell!" she wailed.

Sarah did not know what to say, so she sent a silent prayer to the Lord to give her words that would help this poor confused woman.

Then the Lord brought to her mind Isaiah 55:7:

"Let the wicked forsake his ways, and the unrighteous his own imaginations, and return unto the Lord, and he

> *will have mercy upon him; and to our*
> *God, for he is very ready to forgive.*"

"But He could not forgive such a one as me," Hum-isha-ma protested when Sarah quoted that verse to her. "I have sinned and there is no hope for me," she keened. "I have done great evil, all because I wanted to possess Ebenezer for myself. How can God forgive me for causing the death of those little girls?"

"Hum-isha-ma, that is why Jesus came to earth and gave His life for you, so that your sins could be forgiven. He loves you, Hum-isha-ma, and wants you to know that His forgiveness is freely given. The Bible says that all you have to do is to acknowledge your sins, which you have already done, and

> "*he is faithful and just, to forgive*
> *us our sins, and to cleanse us from all*
> *unrighteousness.*"

"Do you mean that if I do this, I can be forgiven?" Hum-isha-ma asked in astonishment.

"Yes, but you will still have to suffer the consequences of your actions," Sarah explained.

"Then I must die," Hum-isha-ma said sadly.

"Indeed. Unfortunately that is the punishment for murder," Sarah acknowledged.

"Then please pray with me so that I can be forgiven and go to Heaven when I die. I will see Gassisowangen and his family there and tell them I am sorry."

She then bowed her head, and Sarah prayed for her. Hum-isha-ma's eyes lit up with love and peace and Sarah left her, knowing that the angels in Heaven were celebrating over one more soul who would soon be in their presence.

The time came for little Ebenezer to be baptized, and true to their promise to Father Meriel, when he arrived in the spring to meet with Father D' Avaugour, they agreed to let him baptize their son. Thaovenhosen and Sah-teenk-kah were named as his godparents, an honor that they took to heart.

In 1712 France and England reached a preliminary peace when fighting between the two nations drew to a close. Of the approximately 130-140 English captives still remaining in New France, three dozen were from Deerfield. About one third of the Deerfield captives lived in the Indian communities and two-thirds lived with the French. Nine or ten of the Deerfield women who had been young girls when captured had married either French or Indian men and were baptized as Catholics. They had all become naturalized as French subjects, and were not regarded by either the French or Indians as captives, but as citizens. Twenty two of the Deerfield captives had been baptized into the Catholic religion by this time.

In the summer of 1712 Lieutenant Samuel Williams of Deerfield, who was fluent in the French language, led a group of his townsmen to negotiate for the release of the remaining Deerfield captives. Ebenezer's brother John Nims accompanied him to the negotiations with the French governor to try and negotiate Ebenezer and Sarah's release. Two other men from Deerfield joined them to try and negotiate the release of their family members at Kahnawake. They brought a group of French prisoners with them to facilitate an exchange. The party travelled overland starting north in early July and not returning from New France until late September with nine English captives, but Ebenezer and Sarah were not among those who were repatriated.

After the Treaty of Utrecht which ended Queen Anne's War in 1713 was signed, another group of men were commissioned by the Massachusetts council to meet with Governor Vaudreuil to secure the return of all the English captives. Colonel John Stoddard and Reverend John Williams led this group. Their interpreter was Martin Kellogg. Captain Thomas Baker, a former captive, Ebenezer Warner who was searching for his missing daughter, and Jonathan Smith all accompanied them. They left Deerfield headed towards Albany in November of 1713 and hired an Indian named Hendrick, an Iroquois Indian leader to guide them north to Montreal. They had to wait until late January of 1714 for the lakes and rivers to freeze before they could finally set out for New France. They reached Quebec on February 16th, two days after little Ebenezer's birthday.

The men met with Governor Vaudreuil. After they had made their request, he said," All of the remaining captives have the liberty to return and they have my blessing to do so."

Reverend Williams argued, "That's easy for you to say, but the young ones need more than permission to obtain their freedom. They will need intervention by French authorities to gain it."

"Gentlemen, the Natives are our allies. They are not our subjects. Even our king looks at them as such. I cannot force the Indians to deliver their prisoners. However, I see no problems with the French."

When the men from Deerfield discovered that the priests were going from house to house to solicit people to remain in New France, offering them great rewards for staying there, Reverend Williams and Colonel Stoddard protested.

"I could as easily alter the course of the waters as prevent the priests' endeavors," he responded. The men left and sent Captain Baker back to Massachusetts for further instructions, taking only three captives back with him.

Reverend Williams then was able to visit his daughter Eunice who was now married to a Mohawk from Kahnawake. She no longer spoke English, so she said through an interpreter, "I am resolved to live and die here," and looked upon him with disdain. He left her there with great heaviness of heart.

All of the captives who didn't choose to remain in New France were released--that is, all but Ebenezer and Sarah.

In September of 1714 Reverend Williams and Colonel Stoddard along with Martin Kellogg and Thomas Baker arrived in Quebec to arrange for Ebenezer and Sarah to be returned. Father Meriel was in Quebec accompanied by

Father D' Avaugour. When they saw the English ship and realized why the English were in Quebec, they spoke to Governor Vaudreuil about their refusal to release the captives. The governor became very frustrated and shouted, "Ebenezer and Sarah and their son are to be brought to Quebec immediately and they are to come alone without a priest or Indian! I have had enough of this folly!"

"But, the woman is unable to walk this far in her present condition!" Father D' Avaugour objected.

"Then send her on horseback or in a cart, but send her now!" he said in dismissal.

"Yes, your Excellency," they said in surrender.

"I expect to see them no later than tomorrow," Governor Vaudreuil added.

The priests left, but were very distressed with the governor's position. When they arrived back in Lorette, they told Thaovenhosen who went immediately to his wife to tell her of the painful news.

"But they cannot do this to us!" she cried. "They cannot seize our family from us! The baby and the one she now carries are ours!"

"We will follow them and tell them that Ebenezer and Sarah wish to remain here as many of the other captives have done. Even Ebenezer's sister Abigail remains at Sault-au-Récollet. Perhaps we can tell the governor that he wishes to do the same," Thaovenhosen proposed, trying to console his distraught wife.

Ebenezer had overheard Thaovenhosen and Sah-teenk-ka, so he quickly ran home and gathered his wife in his arms. "Sarah, did you know that Reverend Williams and Colonel Stoddard are in Quebec right now trying to secure our release?" he announced. "We can go home soon!"

Sarah couldn't believe the good news, but then reflected, "But how will we tell Thaovenhosen and Sah-teenk-kah that we wish to leave? They will not like to hear this," she worried. "They will be so upset if we leave them."

"I know they will. This is a hard thing to do, but we have always wanted to go home, and I believe that God has finally given us the way to do so," Ebenezer assured her.

"I just don't want to hurt the ones who have treated us like family," Sarah sighed.

"I don't know how I will tell Thaovenhosen of our decision," Ebenezer said. "He does know that Reverend Williams and Colonel Stoddard are in Quebec as Father D' Avaugour and Father Meriel told him the news just a while ago. Thaovenhosen said that he would not let us go because our little Ebenezer is his child too."

"Let us sleep on this," Sarah suggested.

"Let's pray and seek the Lord's guidance, then," Ebenezer responded as he reached for his son who had begun to squirm in Sarah's arms. He sang the little boy's favorite song, Psalm 100 and before he reached the end of singing it, little Ebenezer settled right down and slept soundly, secure in his father's arms.

Ebenezer looked over at his wife, and his eyes shone with love for this woman that he had loved his whole life. How he longed to take her home and build her a home of their own and take care of her and their children. They prayed and then decided that they would not tell Thaovenhosen and Sah-teenk-kah of their eagerness to return for fear that they would not let them go. Ebenezer put little Ebenezer to bed, stirred the fire, and joined his wife to sleep, perhaps, for the last night in their Huron wigwam.

Chapter Thirty Three

"For surely there is an end, and thy hope shall not be cut off."

Proverbs 23:18

I n the morning, just before dawn Ebenezer rose early and led his family away from the village. As they crept away they overheard Thaovenhosen talking to the priests. After hearing the news about Reverend Williams and Colonel Stoddard, Thaovenhosen was saying that he would not let the English men take Ebenezer and his family away.

"We feel the same way," Father Meriel said.

"The child is a French citizen and a Catholic," Father D' Avaugour added.

"I will go now to the Governor and tell him of our agreement that we refuse to release these people who are part of our family here at Lorette," Father Meriel volunteered.

"I will go also," Father D' Avaugour said.

"I must go as well," Thaovenhosen insisted. "They are my family, after all."

Ebenezer and Sarah left the village of Lorette where, except for the few years Sarah had spent living with the de La Rochelles in Montreal, they had lived for ten years as Hurons. They looked across the fields of ripening corn and squash, listened to the roar of the nearby falls, and smelled the surrounding forest and knew that they would always hold this place and these people in their hearts, even though they had to be brought here under such tragic circumstances.

Ebenezer carried his son and Sarah walked alongside, being somewhat weakened because of the heat of the August sun and the fact that she was carrying another baby. When she struggled to keep walking, Ebenezer quoted one of their favorite verses from Isaiah 40:31:

> *"But they that wait upon the Lord,*
> *shall renew their strength: they shall lift*
> *up the wings, as the eagles: they shall*
> *run, and not be weary, and they shall*
> *walk and not faint."*

When they reached the ship, they saw Reverend Williams and Colonel Stoddard talking with Governor Vaudreuil. When the men sighted them, the governor asked, "Have you come alone, then?"

"Yes," Ebenezer replied. "The Lord was with us," Sarah added as she smiled at Ebenezer.

"We were expecting you to come on horseback, or possibly by cart," the governor noted. "The priests and Indians said that you were too weak to travel, Madame Nims. Perhaps they were just using your condition as an excuse," he said as he noted that she seemed to be with child.

"She is as well as women generally are in her condition, but our Lord gave her strength," Ebenezer responded, "but perhaps you will allow us to board so that she may rest?"

"But, of course, he agreed as he helped them into the ship where they would sleep that night before leaving in the morning.

The next day at first light, Thaovenhosen, Sah-teenk-ka, and several of the other Hurons stormed into Quebec and went directly to the ship. They called for Ebenezer and Sarah and demanded that the English men release their family who they felt had been kidnapped. Sah-teenk-ka cried out that she wanted to see her beloved baby Ebenezer. Finally the captain allowed Thaovenhosen and Sah-teenk-ka to board the ship.

"Do you not want to stay with us, your family?" Thaovenhosen asked when they were led to the cabin where Ebenezer and Sarah sat.

"We know that we will miss you and the other people of your village, and we thank you for treating us with kindness," Ebenezer sympathized, "but we want to go home where our English family lives."

"I long to see my mother and sister and brother who live in the Massachusetts colony," Sarah explained. I have not seen them for ten years now."

"But you must leave the child. He is ours. He is a French citizen and has been baptized as a Catholic," Sah-teenk-ka objected. "My heart will break if you take my grandson from me!" she protested.

Sarah handed the sleeping baby to his adopted grandmother who smoothed his golden red hair and kissed his cheek and rocked him back and forth. Sarah's heart ached for her as she also had known loss.

The captain of the ship then interrupted their conversation and told the Indians that they would have to disembark so that they could be on their way.

As the two Indians left the ship, Thaovenhosen comforted his grieving wife with the assurance that he would take her to Deerfield to visit the family the next spring. She reluctantly accepted his attempt to assuage her grief. They stood at the dock with tears running down their cheeks and watched the ship set sail until it disappeared down the river into the rising sun.

The child had awakened when Sah-teenk-ka handed him back to his mother. Ebenezer looked lovingly at his wife and son, both with golden red hair shining in the morning sun and eyes the color of the river, and he thanked God for blessing him abundantly. He remembered Proverbs 13:12 that said,

> *"The hope that is deferred, is the fainting of the heart, but when the desire cometh, it is as a tree of life."*

He had waited so long for his hopes and dreams to be realized, that he could marry his beloved Sarah, that he could have children of his own to love, and that he could bring his family home.

As he reflected on God's immeasurable grace and mercy, his son reached out to him and said, "Sing, Papa, sing a song for me." Ebenezer took him in his arms and sang Psalm 100 for the little boy who held his heart captive. Sarah stood next to them and put her head on his shoulder, joining in the song of praise.

Epilogue

―――――――― ∽ ――――――――

*"But the righteous shall be glad in the
Lord, and trust in him: and all that
are upright of heart, shall rejoice."*

Psalm 64:10

Deerfield, Massachusetts December 1714

S arah had had a wonderful visit with her mother when they arrived in Boston before traveling to Deerfield. She was happy to see that she had survived the rigors of captivity and was happy in her new marriage. When Sarah and Ebenezer and their son finally arrived in Deerfield, they were welcomed back by all of the villagers. Ebenezer's brother John welcomed them into the home that he had rebuilt after the fire that took their little sisters. Ebenezer and Sarah stayed in a two room addition that John had built for Thankful and her husband Benjamin Munn before they were able to finally move into their own permanent home.

This small addition had a fireplace in the main room and a sleeping area at the back. Ebenezer and Sarah were thankful to have a place to live and be close to family.

Sarah spent much time with her sister Mary who had married Judah Wright, one of the captives. Her brother Benjamin who had escaped by jumping through the window and hiding in the corn crib was now a young man. Her beloved brother Jonathan, with whom she had spent so much time in captivity, had made several expeditions to New France to try and secure her release and was now a scout and military officer. He was said to be an expert woodsman, using skills he had acquired while a captive with the Hurons at Lorette. Sarah couldn't believe how much he had grown.

The families were all gathered in the main part of the house to celebrate the first Christmas since their return, after attending church services in the meeting house earlier that day. When they had finished with their meal, Ebenezer left the gathering and went to the back of the house where he and his family lived. He returned with a bundle wrapped in deerskin and handed it to Sarah.

"What is this?" she asked.

"Open it and see," he answered, taking their new baby boy from her lap.

She carefully untied the leather cords binding the bundle and opened it to find the most beautiful pair of leather shoes with fine silver buckles, just like the ones that Ebenezer had made so lovingly more than ten years before.

Ebenezer's eyes gazed tenderly on his family gathered around the fire. He opened Sarah's Bible that her father had given to her when he was led off with the Pennacocks. The book was worn from many years of use, so he handled the precious book with care. Just before he read the Christmas story in Luke chapter two, he quoted from Luke 1:50,

> *"And his mercy is from generation*
> *to generation on them that fear him."*

"Yes, it is, they all agreed, and then they listened as Ebenezer read the familiar Christmas story.

When his father finished the story, little Ebenezer said, "Let's sing the "God the Lord" song. Ebenezer smiled and started singing, but then little Ebenezer ran to the back of the house and grabbed his father's hammer and said, "You tap and sing, Papa!" Ebenezer took the tool from his son and tapped the rhythm as all who were gathered there sang,

"In God the LORD be glad and light.
Praise Him throughout the earth.
Serve Him and come before his sight
With singing and with mirth.
Know that the LORD our God He is.
He did us make and keep.
Not we ourselves for we are His
Own fold and pasture sheep.
O, go into His gates, always
Give thanks within the same.
Within His courts set forth His praise
And laud His holy name.
For why: the goodness of the LORD
Forevermore doth reign.
From age to age throughout the world
His truth doth still remain."

Ebenezer smiled to himself as he remembered his dear little sisters in a time so long ago.

Author's note

My grandmother, who was born in the late 1800's, used to tell me stories of "the olden days" as I'm sure many of my readers' grandmothers did. One of the stories that I loved to hear was about her great, great, great grandparents who were captured by Indians and lived with them for many years. It wasn't until I began researching the genealogical information that became available through the internet that I was able to discover the identity of these ancestors that had so captivated me as a child.

For years, I only had names on a genealogical chart, then after more research I learned of Ebenezer and Sarah's part in the Deerfield Raid of 1704. In 2012 I was thrilled to finally be able to visit Deerfield. This small town has been historically preserved and many of the houses that were not burned during the raid are still standing. The Nims home which is the original house that John Nims and Ebenezer rebuilt after their return now houses a museum which tells the story of the raid. I recommend a visit to this historic town if you would like to experience how life really was during the early 1700's.

Across from the Nims house is the Old Burying Ground which has a mass grave for the residents who were killed in the massacre along with several of the graves of the captives who were able to return. I stood in awe as I read the inscriptions of Ebenezer and Sarah and others of my family whose lives were so changed by that terrible event. After visiting these graves and walking the same street where Ebenezer and Sarah walked more than three centuries before, I knew that I had to write their story.

My sisters have always liked to tease me that they never could believe the truth of any of my stories that I am so fond of relating because, like all writers, I like to embellish things a little to make them more interesting. Although I have taken some liberties with this story, the readers must know that much of it really happened as I have portrayed it.

The town of Deerfield, one of the westernmost settlements in colonial Massachusetts was raided in February, 1704. One hundred eleven residents, including three Frenchmen who had lived in Deerfield for some time were captured and marched through the cold and freezing winter over three hundred miles north to Canada. Ebenezer and Sarah were the last of the captives to be released after more than ten years in captivity. Many of the younger captives, including Ebenezer's sister Abigail and Eunice Williams did remain as French citizens. Although many of the captives died on the march, mostly older women who were pregnant or just having delivered babies like Reverend Williams' wife Eunice and Ebenezer's stepmother Mehitable, and children under the age of three like Sarah's sister Abigail, the majority of those who survived were teenagers and young men who were able to survive the rigorous journey north. Sarah's father David Hoyt did starve to death near present day Keene, New Hampshire after he left with the Pennacocks.

Sarah was not engaged to Joseph Alexander, an actual resident who did escape that first night. Shortly thereafter he married Margaret Mattoon, the sister of Ebenezer's sister Rebecca's husband who was killed in the raid, along with the rest of her family who were either killed or captured.

Sarah didn't live in Montreal with the de La Rochelles, who are fictional characters, as is the infamous Lieutenant Louis St. Germain, but I had to find a way to make Ebenezer a hero who could rescue the damsel in distress! The King's Daughters or *"filles du roi"* were actual historical women as were the soldiers in the *Carignan-Salières.* Sarah and Ebenezer were actually my ancestors on my mother's side, but I was amazed to discover that my father was a descendent of the marriage of a King's Daughter and a soldier from the *Carignan-Salières!* Further research revealed that the soldier was actually from La Rochelle, France, a place I had chosen at random before learning of my father's ancestor from that town! I have based the character of Madame Charon, the French woman who gave the captives refuge and food when they arrived at Fort Chambly on another of my father's ancestors who was born at Fort Chambly and lived there at the time of the captives' arrival.

Of course there was no duel between Ebenezer and Lieutenant St. Germain, but, according to several accounts, the priests did try to force Sarah to marry a French officer and she did object in public, declaring that she would marry, but not a Frenchman. When she proclaimed that she would only marry a captive if any would have her, Ebenezer quickly gained courage and stepped up and volunteered. They were married by the astonished Father Meriel on the spot, but he insisted that as a condition for him allowing the marriage that any children would be baptized as Catholics. Many years later, when their son Ebenezer Junior was in his twenties, he was baptized anew by Reverend John Ashley, the new minister of Deerfield and went on to fight in many future battles with the Natives and French.

A great deal of this story centers around the conflict not only between the French and English, but also between the two opposing religious traditions, Protestant Puritanism and Roman Catholicism as well as the various alliances with the Natives.

The description of Ebenezer and Sarah's final escape was as I recorded. The Hurons of Lorette were the most Christianized of all the Natives and did develop deep bonds with their captives. For the most part, they treated them not as captives, but as family members and Thaovenhosen and his wife were devastated by the loss of their adopted family.

The great chief Tsawenhohi and Thaovenhosen were actual men. Thaovenhosen was a much respected Christian Huron and made several trips to Deerfield after the captives were released to visit them. In fact, his visitations became so frequent that Sarah's brother Jonathan Hoyt actually had to petition the Massachusetts court for relief from taxes because of the expense of feeding and housing him! The incident where he saved Jonathan's life during the Mourning War controversy on the march did occur. Gassisowangen was based on the real Huron warrior, name unknown, who wanted to kill him to avenge their Great Chief's life. Hum-isha-ma is a fictional character as are all the events regarding her. The little girls, Hatironda and Kondiaronk, are also the author's creations.

Fathers Meriel, and D' Avaugour were actual priests in Montreal and Lorette and much of the records of marriages, births, and baptisms of the captives were meticulously recorded by Father Meriel.

The names of the dead and captives were all as recorded by Reverend Williams in his book, *"The Redeemed Captive Returning to Zion: a Faithful History of Remarkable Occurrences in the Captivity and Deliverance of Mr. John Williams,"* which he published in 1707 after his release, and, yes, it was made possible because the English did release the notorious pirate Baptiste!

John Nims' daring escape is as portrayed. The story of Godfrey Nims that he related to his son Ebenezer about wanting to run away to the French in Canada with John Bennet and Benoni Stebbins when they were lads in Northampton did occur as related and can be found in the court records of that time.

The story of Mary Webster (also one of the author's relatives by marriage) was as recorded. Her husband was a descendent of my ancestor Governor John Webster, one of the first governors of Connecticut. Governor Webster was also one of the authors of the Connecticut constitution, which served as a model for the United States Constitution. As an aside, one of the judges in the infamous Salem witch trials was also a relative, but that's another story!

After living with John Nims for a few years in the family home, Ebenezer and Sarah moved to the small village of Wapping a few miles south of Deerfield where they lived a quiet life, raising six sons and living to a ripe old age.

To further my research, my husband and I revisited Deerfield and after touring the historic houses and museums there, we drove the route that the captives travelled to Montreal. We stopped at Fort Chambly and toured the exhibit of the Deerfield raid, and saw the actual snowshoes that the captives had worn and one of the sleds that carried the children. It was a sobering experience to see these items that my ancestors and other captives had used more than 300 years earlier.

From there we boarded a cruise ship to Boston, stopping in Quebec City and visiting the actual recreated Huron Village at Lorette. I was so thankful for our Huron guide who explained how life was in their village at the time of the Ebenezer and Sarah's stay there. The longhouse and other structures were as they were at that time and seeing them allowed me to recreate some of the events that happened in my story. It was an invaluable experience that will long live in my memory along with that of walking the streets of Deerfield which remain much the same as they were on that fateful morning in 1704.

I would be remiss if I didn't share with the reader the sources that helped me in my research. I must give credit to C. Alice Baker for much of the material on which this book is based for her exhaustive study on the Deerfield captivity in her book, *True Stories of New England Captives* published in 1897. Her mother's family had ties to Deerfield and in the 1840's she attended Deerfield Academy, where she later returned to teach. She moved to Deerfield and purchased the Frary House, her ancestral home and restored it, later founding the Pocumtuck Valley Memorial Association which also provided much of the material for this book.

I must thank Sally Phillips, from the Flynt House Museum in Deerfield, who is a descendant of Ebenezer's sister Thankful Nims for her valuable help in learning more about life in Deerfield three hundred years ago.

Additional References

Haefeli, Evan and Sweeney, Kevin, *Captors and Captives: The 1704 French and Indian Raid on Deerfield,* Massachusetts University of Massachusetts Press, 2003

Oathout, Susan S., Schultz, John H., and Suddaby, Elizabeth C. *The Nims Family: Seven Generations of Descendants from Godfrey Nims.* Greenville, SC: *Southern Historical Press, Inc.,1990*

Demos, John, *The Unredeemed Captive: A Family Story From Early America, New York: Vintage Books,1995*

New England Captives Carried to Canada, Emma L. Coleman, 1925

David W. Hoyt, A Genealogical History of the Hoyt, Haight, and Hight Families, (Boston,1871).

The Whole Book of Psalmes: With the Hymnes Evangelicall, and Songs Spiritual 1621, Cantus Simon Stubbs version 1621

The History of Deerfield, Vol. I, George Sheldon, 1895,

Judd, S. 1905. History of Hadley. H. R. Hunting, Springfield.

Mappen, M. 1980. Witches & Historians. Robert E. Krieger Publishing Company, Huntingdon, N.Y.

Mayo, L. S. 1936. *The History of the Colony and Province of Massachusetts-Bay by Thomas Hutchinson. Harvard University Press, Cambridge.*

Mather, C. 1967. *Magnalia Christi Americana. Vol. II, Russell & Russell, New York.*

In addition to the published works, I am indebted to the following online resources:

https://www.biblegateway.com
www.wendake.ca/nation
http://www.historic-deerfield.org/deerfield.html
www.ancestry.com
www.ehow.com
http://wmich.edu/fortstjoseph/docs/panels/women-new-france.pdf
http://www.bio.umass.edu/biology/conn.river/witch.html
www.maplemuseum.com
www.museehuronwendat.ca
www.totatsga.org huron history
www.newadvent.org
www.catholic.org/encyclopedia/

Reader's Guide Questions

1. This is a story about conflict between nations, religious beliefs and customs, and relationships between individuals. What is your response to Sarah's decision to attend the party at the de la Rochelle's and dance with the insistent Lieutenant St. Germain?

2. Should Sarah have stuck to her Puritan belief that it was wrong to attend such an event, or was she right in feeling that she must obey the wishes of her mistress?

3. Have you ever faced a situation where whichever decision you had to make involved compromising your belief in what was right in the eyes of the Lord?

4. Were the Massachusetts authorities wise to finally release the privateer Baptiste in order to secure the release of Reverend John Williams?

5. What were some of the ramifications of Thaovenhosen's action in releasing Jonathan to

the English for money, both immediately and long term?

6. Do you think that Ebenezer's father Godfrey Nims died of his wounds or from a broken heart? What effect did the guilt he felt over his youthful actions have on his death?

7. Why do you think some of the captives decided to stay in New France instead of seeking to return to their homes in Deerfield?

8. Why do you think Sarah and Ebenezer decide to leave their home in Lorette with the Hurons who had adopted them into their families?

9. Ebenezer and his father Godfrey were cordwainers or shoemakers. What were the various types of footwear worn, and how did they each play a part in the story?

About the author

———— ⌒⌒ ————

Joyce Dent Morgan has always enjoyed searching her family history and reading about the events that were happening to her family during their lifetimes. Sometimes a story unfolds that just has to be shared, and she just has to write it.

She has been married to her high school sweetheart for more than fifty years. They have two sons, five grandchildren, and one great-granddaughter. They have lived in several states and enjoy exploring the local scenic areas and making new friends. She currently lives in Southern Nevada.